COLD AS STONE

LISA HUGHEY

LISA HUGHEY

COLD AS STONE

A Family Stone Romantic Suspense Novel
by Lisa Hughey

October 2015

Lisa Hughey

Ebook ISBN: 978-0-9964352-2-2

Print ISBN: 978-1-950359-01-1

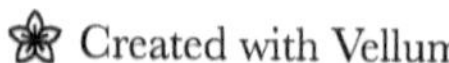 Created with Vellum

For survivors everywhere.

PROLOGUE

John Pulaski stood in the small hospital chapel. The scratchy wool blend of his Dress Blues was stiff and formal against the scars of his mangled knee and prosthetic leg.

A small unadorned urn sat upon the marble steps. Multi-colored light bathed the entire room in warmth and beauty. The intimate worship chamber was remarkably pretty, with a fancy stained-glass window in jewel tones that portrayed a nondenominational scene depicting doves and a rising sun.

Mom would have liked this. The random thought broke through the thick fog that seemed to surround him, as if he were wading through an emotional soup of regret, grief, and finally, a burning cold rage.

All his life, he'd asked about his dead father. All his life, she'd spun tales of a heroic soldier KIA. Her stories of his father were the reason he'd enlisted. The reason he'd done many things in his thirty-five years. He'd become a Marine because of her stories about a hero.

But on her deathbed, her body ravaged by the cancer

that had slowly eaten away at her flesh and bones, a husk of the woman who'd raised him—who'd nurtured him onto the path of becoming the man he was, especially with her many tales of a father who was larger than life—she had confessed.

With one simple, emotionally complicated sentence she'd rocked his world. Because it turned out those tales were just that. Fiction.

As she lay dying, she'd told him the truth: his father wasn't dead. Then she begged him to find the man.

His father wasn't a dead war hero. He was just an asshole who'd abandoned his mother when she was pregnant and left her to struggle and scrimp her whole adult life when he apparently had millions. He was a multimillionaire who could have provided his mother with superior healthcare and treatment for the cancer that finally took her.

John couldn't give a shit for himself, because it had always been him and mom against the world. But a frigid rage stole over him as he lowered onto the hard, wood pew and laid his mother to rest. No big funeral, she hadn't wanted it, couldn't have afforded it and hadn't wanted him to spend his savings giving her one.

His mother hadn't asked for much. She'd saved everything for her son. Even when he was finally able to take care of her, she'd continued to give as much as she could to John.

Her final request? His mom, bizarrely, wanted him to find his father so he wouldn't be all alone in the world. John mentally snorted. He wasn't alone. Exactly.

But after being honorably discharged after a roadside IED had rolled his Humvee, killed a civilian contractor, and taken his left leg from the knee down, he was definitely adrift. He'd promised his mother. So he'd look for the sperm donor who'd fathered him but never bothered to care for his mother. John hadn't promised to be nice. He'd promised only to find him.

John sat in the unnervingly quiet silence and plotted. His entire world was frozen by the realization that his mother had died broke because she couldn't afford health insurance because of Jackson Stone Sr. Yeah, he had a few things to say to Jack Stone.

His heart was as cold as the stone floor beneath his feet as he considered his next move. He'd find his father. Give him a piece of his mind. Then he'd start the rest of his life. If he didn't know what that entailed yet, no problem. He was a Marine. *Ooh rah.*

John bent his head and promised his mother. Always faithful.

He had idolized and revered his father his whole life. Lived up to that image of his father. Lived up to the ideals that were suddenly a lie.

So what did he believe in now? Who did he admire? Going forward, how did he live his live with integrity when the foundation was rotten?

CHAPTER 1

S*ix months later*

Sɪɴ Cɪᴛʏ ᴡᴀs hot as hell. John Pulaski strode down the crowded Las Vegas Strip, his knee and stump swollen and achy. Immense heat shimmered off the sidewalk in mirage-like waves, the high temperature causing his knee joint to swell. The silicone liner that covered his residual limb—and prevented his prosthetic leg from completely rubbing the already mutilated skin raw—was soggy with sweat. The swollen stump meant he really needed an ice bath and a shot of scotch. Instead he was trolling the streets of Vegas, on a mission to help his half-brother, Jack.

He wondered how he'd gone from a place of anger and revenge against his absent, asshole father to having an instant family.

One minute he'd been ringing the doorbell to a huge mansion in Monterey, California, waiting with trepidation and not a little bit of rage, not sure what he was going to say to the man who'd knocked up and then abandoned his mother, but gearing up for a confrontation.

The next minute he had a ready-made family of grown-up siblings, their significant others, and a surrogate mom who was in actuality only a few years older than him.

Jackson Stone Jr., his half-brother, had been determined to bring John into their odd little family fold. This job was a trial mission for both of them.

John would see how he liked working for his brother's companies, Global Humanitarian Relief and Stone Consulting. Global Humanitarian Relief was a privately funded disaster relief and humanitarian aid company, and performed missions all over the world. Their charter was to give aid wherever necessary. Although nothing had been revealed, John was pretty sure that Stone Consulting's operations dealt in more covert purposes. Both possibilities appealed to him.

With this op, Jack would be able to assess if John was a good fit for either company.

When Jack had asked him to come to work with them, John had been hesitant. He had to admit the job sounded pretty awesome, and after all what else was he going to do?

He'd been offered an administrative job with the Marines but he was used to doing, not sitting behind a desk. The thought of not being active had turned his stomach.

So here he was working a temp job for his brother.

Eight years ago, four girls had been abducted. They'd been on their way from school to the fields so they could work and help support their families. For eight long years, the case had remained unsolved. No leads. Until a few months ago, when Maria Torres had escaped her imprisonment and told the world what José Fernandez had done.

Maria had been imprisoned and left alive for eight years.

One of the girls had died after being raped.

The remaining two girls were still missing. No one had seen them since they'd been abducted.

They finally had a lead on the missing girls which was why they were in Vegas.

This first mission was turning out to be a lot different than he'd anticipated. In the Marines he'd worked with a unit. They knew each other's foibles and fears. They respected each other and worked together with a clear chain of command.

On this job, his team consisted of three members. Him. Maria Torres. And Marissa Evans. Maria was the former kidnap victim and eight-year hostage who was still adjusting to a world that didn't consist of only herself. Marissa "Ball Buster" Evans was a borderline hostile operative who worked with Jack's fiancée at an image consulting firm. But today, at least, Marissa wasn't playing nice.

John had only met Marissa yesterday. She'd taken over registering at the hotel, ordered him to take the larger bedroom, and generally bossed him around. Then today, she'd insisted that they needed to take Maria shopping. She needed to have clothes that blended in the Vegas scene.

John had suggested that Marissa and Maria go together. But that had been an even bigger no-go than not shopping at all. Marissa Evans had shut him down with one fierce look. So here they were walking the Strip after spending the last hour at the mall.

While Marissa hadn't said anything outright, he could sense her irritation with the situation, her aggravation with him, at least it seemed that way, and some other indefinable emotion emanating from her. She'd simmered all morning and now marched ahead of him and Maria in the thickening afternoon crowd on the Vegas strip.

To add insult to injury, she was hot. Way hot. Way-out-of-his-league, even before he was missing half a leg, hot. And for some reason everything was bothering him, the heat, his leg, Maria's stress, Marissa's irritation, and the fact that a woman like her wouldn't look at him once, let alone twice, and he could feel his temper rising.

He never lost his temper when he'd been active duty.

He was known for his cool under pressure. But his calm was unraveling with every tick up the thermometer and every snippy click of Marissa's four-inch heels.

People everywhere, tourists of all shapes and sizes and colors, cluttered the sidewalks. Different languages--English, Dutch, German, Cantonese, Japanese, Korean, French, Southern, New England, Surfer--assaulted his ears. Frenetic walkers and leisurely gawkers, tourists who stopped mid-stride to snap selfies, short, tall, fat, skinny, happy, angry—it seemed as if the entire population of Vegas was on this particular section of the Strip.

For a few minutes, focused on his own discomfort and total sense of disconnect with reality, he'd zoned out, thinking Maria was in better hands with a woman, since her imprisonment had been carried out by men. Because of his inattention, he'd missed the signs that Maria was having a mini-freak-out.

Marissa was on point. Maria was in the middle. John had positioned himself in the rear, to Maria's left and slightly behind her so that he could watch her six and keep his focus on their surroundings. But now his attention zoomed in on Maria. She clutched her shopping bags in her left hand so tightly her light brown fingers were white with a lack of blood. Her steps had become more and more jerky, and he could see the bright shine of sweat on her face. He was pretty sure it wasn't because she was affected by the soaring desert temps.

He wasn't thrilled with the number of people on the street either. It made it difficult to guard Maria and pay attention to anyone else who might be paying too much attention to them. Not likely but still he needed to be on alert.

Of course, Miss BB, John's pet name for Marissa, was too far ahead to get her attention. However he couldn't wait until Marissa figured out they were lagging behind. They were almost at the steps of Caesar's Palace when John curled his fingers around Maria's bicep. She jerked, then held still. Small tremors skittered through her. He could literally feel her fear through the clasp of his hand. He leaned in to whisper in her ear. He hated to spook her by getting too close, but the street was actually loud enough it would be difficult to hear him otherwise. "You okay?"

"Crowd" was all she whispered, but it was enough for John.

"Come on." He tugged her toward the curved portico in front of Caesar's and into the shadows. He tucked her into the small corner so she was out of the traffic on the sidewalk. People still headed toward stairs and the entrance to the casino but this spot was far less hectic.

Her breathing was becoming more and more erratic. He was hoping she wasn't going to completely hyperventilate. "Hang on, *chica*. We'll get you out."

John glanced over his shoulder at Marissa. She'd finally realized they weren't behind her and had turned around to search the sidewalk.

She found them quickly, and her gaze locked on his. He

lifted his chin, noted the tightening of her luscious mouth. Dammit. He must be one sick SOB to be attracted to a woman who couldn't stand him. Yeah, she was hot, but he was too smart and too old to get drawn in by a smokin' body and gorgeous face with a shitty attitude.

BB strode toward them like she was on a mission, like she wanted to break his balls and eat them for breakfast. She could be pissed at him all she wanted but Maria needed to be treated with care.

John raised an eyebrow.

"Problem?" she asked quietly. And thank Christ, she'd toned down the attitude. Maria didn't need any more strife.

Maria was bent over while John rubbed her back. "Too many people."

Marissa glanced around as if noting all avenues of escape. "I'll get the car."

"I can—"

"Don't. I said I'll go get the car."

Yep, Ball Buster. He'd spent a sum total of three hours in her presence and she barely tolerated him. The next few days were going to be…difficult.

"Let's see if Maria can walk to the garage." John overruled her. "Otherwise, we have to wade into the crowd again for you to pick us up."

The traffic on the Strip was insane and the garage wasn't that far away.

Marissa crossed her arms over her very generous chest. Round handfuls plumped as her mannish white broadcloth blouse gaped at the button. He didn't think she'd appreciate it if he pointed that out. Her wide-leg navy pants and suit jacket screamed Fed, even though according to Jack she worked at Adams-Larsen. Which was ostensibly an image consulting firm. So exclusive they refused to name their clients. They guaranteed absolute and total confidentiality.

But John had to believe that there was more to the firm than spinning politicians' personal reputations and celebrity's social media postings. Why? Because otherwise, Marissa Evans's presence on this mission made no sense whatsoever.

Her startling aquamarine gaze dropped to John's hand as he continued to try to soothe their reluctant companion. He'd hated the idea of bringing Maria to Vegas. Had argued against it in fact.

But the truth was, Maria Torres was one of the few women who actually knew the targets. And if they found them, she might be the only one able to get through to these women. Assuming they could find them.

Once Maria had escaped from her solitary prison, they'd been able to finally arrest the man who had been behind the kidnappings. A local social activist who had wanted to make a name for himself, José Fernandez. Until he'd been arrested, Fernandez was a pillar of the community and considered a champion of farm workers' rights. A veritable God in the Latinx population.

Supposedly José Fernandez had no idea what had happened to the two remaining girls. But he had finally, *finally* given the gag-ordered grand jury a name, Manuel Ortega, when it was clear that the only way he was going to reduce his own jail time was to cough up the accomplice.

They had age-progression photos of the girls', now women's, appearance. If by some chance they found the two women who'd been abducted with her, Maria was the one who might get them to talk. Assuming they were even in Las Vegas. Assuming they weren't completely traumatized by whatever had happened to them. Assuming they were still alive.

It was a hell of a lot of assuming.

"You okay to walk to the car?" John bent over to ask her and his pants rode up, exposing the ankle joint of his prosthetic leg.

He heard the small gasp that the Ball Buster hadn't been able to suppress. If she started being nice now, he'd be the one chewing glass and throwing dark glares. He would never fucking play the sympathy card. His leg, or lack thereof, was just a fact of his life, nothing more.

Fortunately Maria answered, "Yes." She stood and straightened her shoulders resolutely. Her swarthy face was pale, and about every third breath was a tight gasp, but her cinnamon-and- chocolate eyes radiated determination. "I can make it."

Pride welled in John's chest. She was a fucking survivor. And BB was going to respect that or she was gone. He didn't care how she treated him, but she needed to show Maria the deference she deserved.

"Of course you can," John said. Her unbreakable spirit shone through. If eight years of captivity with only a television and herself for company didn't break her, she could handle the crowded streets of Las Vegas.

"Close protection format," John instructed Marissa, who'd watched the quick exchange with a stoic expression.

"Okay."

He wondered what the hell her deal was. But that was a mystery for later.

"Maria, you stay between us. We'll protect you." Marissa's voice had lowered, gentled, and she seemed almost compassionate when she spoke to the other woman.

"Thank you." Maria's mouth tipped up and John was

happy to see that color was returning to her cheeks and her breathing was already easier.

He patted Maria's shoulder. "You'll be okay."

Marissa stared at his hand on Maria's shoulder for a long second. Then she jingled the rental keys in long fingers tipped with no-nonsense, short and unpainted nails. "Let's go," she said curtly.

Ball Buster was back.

CHAPTER 2

C*ould she be more of a bitch?*

Probably not. All Rissa wanted to do was bury her head in the fluffy pillow on her bed and be miserable for the next hundred years.

John Pulaski had patted Maria on the shoulder to comfort her, and all Rissa had wanted was for the same attention from the hulking former Marine. A moment in his large, muscled biceps so she could get her shit together and go on.

Because dammit, she hadn't wanted this assignment. She wasn't ready. Her damn head was still fucked up.

Yet her boss had sent her to Las Vegas to help John Pulaski and Stone Consulting track down two women who were abducted eight years ago. She wasn't ready for a partner, she wasn't ready to be in the field, and she damn sure wasn't ready to watch over one traumatized victim.

She identified far more with the victim—and yes she fucking hated that word—than the protector.

Instead of being able to put herself in some sort of quit-losing-it timeout by hiding in her bed, she had to hang out in the common area of the suite.

Maria needed some time alone, which Rissa got, she really did. They were housed in an off-Strip hotel in a three-room suite. A common area with a full kitchen, table, and living room was flanked by two bedrooms. The main bedroom had a king-size bed and Jacuzzi tub while the other bedroom sported two queen beds and a nice bathroom.

There should have been enough room for them all, even if they were virtual strangers.

Unfortunately, the three-room, two-bedroom, two-bathroom suite felt way too small while Maria was locked away with a cold cloth over her head and the curtains drawn in the bedroom they were sharing.

Rissa gently closed the connecting door between her and Maria's bedroom and the living area.

The tension headache that throbbed behind her left eye was getting worse. When she'd been on the Strip, she'd been doing okay in the straight sections, crowded but not too bad. But when she'd hit the street corner and the people started piling up waiting for the light to change, her mind had gone to another place. Her breath had shortened, as if she could draw in only tiny sips of air, and all her doubts and fears had pinged around her brain like those balls banging around in the lotto machine, bouncing off each other in a frantic mess. And suddenly, she had needed to get out of there. Away from the press of humanity.

She could empathize with Maria's panic. But Rissa hadn't even noticed. She'd been too caught up in her own drama to see that Maria was having similar issues. Dammit. So freaking unprofessional.

She was *not* ready to be back in the field.

The living room was blessedly empty. She needed to apologize to John but that would have to wait until he was around. Right now she could relax in peace.

That was when she noticed that the sliding door to their third-story balcony was open about an inch. She could see John's silhouette through the filmy curtains that hid the interior of the suite from prying eyes.

John Pulaski was, physically, just her type. His black hair sprinkled with gray was just long enough brush his ears and collar. His face was all angles and lines, a long nose with a bump on the bridge, high cheekbones, and a strong uncompromising clean-shaven jaw. He had thick shoulders, a large chest, and thighs the size of the palm trees lining the Strip. His chest tapered in to his waist and led to a world-class ass. She hadn't had any idea that he was also missing part of his left leg until this afternoon. Something no one bothered to mention to her.

Then she wondered why she thought she had any right to know his business. She certainly didn't want to share hers with anyone.

Ugh, if he was out there, she needed to apologize.

She wanted to have this conversation about as much as she wanted to be in the field. But she wasn't about to back away from an uncomfortable few moments. She did have her pride. Truth be told, she probably had too much pride. But that was inconsequential right this minute.

Rissa eased the slider open and stepped out onto the small balcony. The old Las Vegas Hotel, newly named Westgate something or other but everyone still called it the LVH, was to their left. She focused on that giant sign rather than stare directly at John.

The wall of heat hit like a three-hundred-pound

linebacker, making it momentarily hard to breathe. This dry heat was so very different from the humid soup of DC, but so hot it could sear your lungs. As she sucked in air, she inhaled cigarette smoke.

And her apology disintegrated when the acrid odor hit her brewing migraine.

She turned her head sharply and glared at him. "That's a filthy habit," she said. Anger and shame roiled in her stomach because she was giving him a hard time.

Something about this man and nearly every move he made caused her to want to strike out, strike back. As a result, she had been a flaming bitch all day, but she couldn't seem to stop.

"True." His perfectly formed lips wrapped around the white tip as he sucked the nicotine into his lungs. She was mesmerized by the sensual curve of his mouth, and the absolute lack of remorse as he blew the smoke right in her face. "You're welcome to leave."

Her gaze flicked to his lips, then back up to his darkened eyes, the hazel taking on more of the color of the whiskey in his glass. God, she was such a bitch.

Rissa shunted her attention to the chairs on the balcony, the slightly opened sliding glass door that shielded their charge from view, the curl of smoke in the air, anywhere but on the serious, pissed-off man whose commanding presence filled the airspace around them with a pulsing masculine energy.

Her traitorous body reacted to that testosterone-laden vibe. She didn't feel threatened by him, instead she had that "I want to rip your clothes off" heightened awareness that had her hormones on red alert.

She didn't understand him. She didn't understand her

reaction to him either. For the most part, men didn't affect her. She could take them or leave them. Of course, she'd taken plenty when she'd been trying to drown out the noise in her head after the incident. But sleeping with every man who crossed her path hadn't helped. And she'd gone back to being her more typically reclusive self.

Rissa dropped into one of the painted metal chairs, and pressed her knees together, wishing she could rest her forehead on her knees. It would be so very unprofessional to curl into a fetal ball and start rocking back and forth. But something about this man had every one of her defenses going on alert and she was terrified to relax her guard around him. She took a deep breath, straightened up, and forced herself to look him in the eyes. "I apologize."

"For what?" He wasn't being dense. He just wanted to make her say it. She could see his refusal to let her off easy in his narrowed gaze. She appreciated his insistence to hold her accountable, even as she was tempted to bash him over the head for making her voice it out loud.

But there was more to his perusal. The annoyance in his gaze was layered with heat. The sexual pull between them was difficult to ignore when she could tell he was feeling it too.

Fine, he could be as annoyed as he wanted. She wasn't about to air all her secrets, but she also needed to acknowledge her bitchy attitude. Then she realized she had no idea how to explain without actually explaining. Rissa hesitated, wondering just what she could or would share, and kicking herself for not figuring out earlier exactly how she was going to handle disseminating information without baring her soul and her mistakes.

She'd been so concerned about the handling the weapons segment of this assignment that she'd completely forgotten she'd have to deal with the emotional impact of just…being on the job. As he blew another stream of smoke toward her, she abandoned those thoughts. Screw it, she'd apologized. As far as she was concerned, that was the end of it.

If he could be a dick, then she'd just continue to be a bitch. Not a very mature attitude but fuck it. Now that she'd gotten that out of the way, they needed to focus on logistics.

So she shifted the conversation to the job. "Let's talk strategy."

His left hand rested on his left knee, the cigarette held comfortably between his index and middle finger. He stayed silent, watching her like a hawk waiting for the mouse to give away its position. She refused to be a scared mouse. He lifted one of the kitchen glasses to his lips. The amber liquid rocked in the glass as he took a healthy slug. Smoke curled lazily in the air between them. She watched the muscles in his throat move when he swallowed and her mouth went desert dry.

"We can't keep dragging Maria around. She can't handle it," Rissa said sharply.

"Cut her some slack. She's dealing with a lot of stuff."

Weren't they all? She threw up her hands. "I wasn't being critical. I don't want her to have to handle it." Rissa huffed out an irritated breath. "I am not the enemy."

He merely raised an eyebrow and wrapped those sinful lips around the cigarette again. It was a filthy habit. So why was she so aroused by the simple purse of his lips as she imagined him sucking on other, more intimate, things with as much force.

Jesus. She was losing what was left of her mind.

Rissa licked her lips as her nipples tightened and heat pooled low in her belly. "We're on the same side here."

"Are we?" he asked neutrally.

Frustration, fierce and sharp, stabbed at her head, but she resisted the urge to rub the back of her neck. "Of course we are."

Just because she wasn't sure she could handle the emotional pressure of being in the field again didn't mean that the effort wasn't worthwhile. It just meant that she didn't know how she was going to hold up. But he didn't know anything about her problems, and his passive-aggressive needling guaranteed that unless she somehow put him in danger, he wasn't going to know.

It was her weakness, her problem, and she'd be the one to deal with it.

John eyed Marissa through the screen of smoke. Dusk was starting to fall, painting the sky an artistic mix of pastel blues, pinks and yellows.

"What do you suggest?" he finally asked.

"Anything that keeps her safe and in her comfort zone."

"Agreed."

The intelligence they had so far indicated that Manuel Ortega was the man who had brokered the deal for the girls. But he was a shadowy figure, a resident of Mexico who traveled to the US regularly for business. He had plenty of legitimate businesses, and until his name came up in the search for these girls, there had been very little chatter about any illegal dealings.

Ortega owned a high-end strip club in Vegas. For the first time, there was a hint that there was more beneath the surface of the legal façade of the club. The reason they'd put together this op so quickly is because they found out that Ortega was in Vegas right now.

It was possible that the kidnapped girls had been forced into prostitution. On paper, in any computer records, the link between José Fernandez, the disgraced politician, and Manuel Ortega was nonexistent.

Until Fernandez had given up Ortega's name.

If Fernandez hadn't fingered the businessman, the investigation would still be in the dark and a total dead end. Fernandez had denied any additional involvement in the kidnapping of the four girls. He'd insisted that he didn't know what had happened to them after his guys had handed them over to Ortega. But Jack Stone was convinced that the SOB was lying.

She didn't know why Jack thought the girls might be in Vegas. However if Jack's information indicated a connection between the missing women and this club, Rissa was going to follow up on it. Even if every lead went nowhere, Rissa would spend the time to track it because those girls deserved justice.

"What if we check out the strip club?" She wanted to go to a strip club with John Pulaski about as much as she wanted to fire her weapon again. She kept all reluctance out of her voice. "We could leave Maria here tonight and take a field trip."

The earthy peaty scent of fine liquor lingered in the hot air.

John took another sip of scotch and eyed her over the rim of the glass. "You want to go to the strip club." He hadn't made it sound like a question, more of a derisive statement.

She knew what she looked like. Uptight. Prim. Overly proper. Those words described exactly how she'd been acting. But dammit. Even with her limitations she was a capable, sharp investigator or her boss, Jillian Larsen, would have never sent her on this mission.

She ignored the fact that he doubted her. After all, she

had doubts about herself. But she'd never admit that to anyone. Most especially John freaking Pulaski.

Her stomach sloshed at the thought of doing undercover reconnaissance with him. Not just him, any partner.

He flicked ash into the little black tray, and glanced at her almost mannish blouse and boring navy pants. "You need a different wardrobe."

The tailored suit and plain blouse were her armor, engineered to make her seem competent, in control. Exactly what she had been…before. Back when it wasn't armor but just her uniform. Now she employed the motto: Fake it 'til you make it.

She'd come prepared for undercover work even though the idea had her waking up in a sweat and wanting to toss her dinner.

"I've got appropriately slutty clothes." She fought to keep her voice level, even as she felt his gaze on her chest, lingering.

And those inappropriate feelings were back. Stronger than ever. Her girl parts tingled and her head went a little light.

"Only if we can get a babysitter for Maria." John shifted back into business mode, his face blank, and his warm eyes went flat, cool. He stubbed out the butt in the plastic ashtray on the little glass end table between their chairs. "I am not leaving her alone tonight."

That protective streak of his was damn attractive. And while *she* could take care of herself, she appreciated his instinct to care for others weaker than himself.

He was right. Maria was frightened by the crowds and lights and noise. Understandably so. She'd been alone with only her own company for eight years. A cruel form of solitary confinement. The last time Adams-Larsen had been in charge of Maria there had been problems. Problems like Maria freaked and bolted. She had trouble trusting people. Not surprising.

"She's got some serious balls," Rissa said wistfully, remembering back to the time when she had considerable mission mojo. Now her moxie was gone. It had disappeared in a puff of cordite when her partner coded on the floor of a dirty warehouse.

John smirked. His lips pursed like he was holding back something. Then suddenly a chuckle escaped, his mouth curved, his cheeks puffed and mirth sparkled in his eyes. A laugh erupted sounding like it was from deep in his belly and he bent over.

"What the hell is so funny?"

"Nothing, BB."

"Just call me Rissa." She wasn't at all sure she wanted to know what BB stood for.

This whole mission was like one great big test of her mental stability.

She knew for a fact that this job was a trial mission for him. If it went well, he would join Jack Stone's company. He likely couldn't afford to fuck up either.

John wiped at his wet eyes.

"You going to explain that?" He wasn't laughing at her. Somehow she knew that instinctively but his obvious amusement was irritating as hell.

He studied her for another second. "Nope."

Rissa didn't want to let Jillian down. On the surface, Adams-Larsen was an image consulting firm which they did in a very limited capacity. In reality, their agency helped people disappear legally, whether they were the target of stalking, or threats from exes, or other forms of harassment.

Last month they even helped a whistleblower set up a new life free from worry about being harassed.

They didn't *find* missing people. Sure, in theory they could work backward, but it wasn't really their strength. And since she'd been out of the game, in the office working as the receptionist and doing research, for over two years, she was more liability than asset.

Rissa's heart thudded hard and frantic in her chest. She could barely worry about herself let alone another person. What if she couldn't handle a situation or something happened and she had a flashback?

She cursed her boss, but whining about her fears wasn't going to change her mission. Time to get back to it.

"All we really have are the age progression photos, and a very vague tip from Fernandez. Manuel Ortega's strip club is one of many in the city."

"Jack has been digging further into Ortega's network investigating for new information." His voice was mild.

"I still feel like it was premature to come to Las Vegas and start with only two sketchy pieces of evidence." Her frustration at her own very real issues made her voice sharp and her throat tight. Sweat sheened on her brow. Her stomach twisted and whirled like the roller coaster on top of New York-New York. Her doubts crowded in again.

But Rissa kept her chin up, shoulders squared, and mentally projected an air of efficient competence, refusing to show any weakness in front of John freaking Pulaski.

"Doesn't matter what we think." John drained the amber liquid from the glass, placed it deliberately on the little table between them, and then stretched his arms over his head and his legs out in front of him. The move lifted his cotton polo and exposed a strip of ripped flesh at his waist. His abs were a work of art. His shoulders popped and his biceps bulged straining the ribbed cotton hem of his polo shirt.

And her head went light.

"We're not in charge of this op. Jack is." He dropped his arms and rubbed at his knee. The one with the prosthetic below it. Her heart squeezed tightly. She could already tell that he wouldn't want her sympathy. So she didn't ask if he was okay, even if she wanted to. Badly.

However, she hated the fact that he was so blasé about their serious lack of intel.

"So you just blindly follow orders?" Her bitch was back. Not really his fault. Except he was so damn calm. So damn low energy. So damn accepting.

"He's my CO on this job," he said mildly. "And it's my first for Stone Consulting."

"Why'd he have *you* do this?" Based on what she knew of the Stone family, they had a whole lot more personally invested in this mission than a potential new employee who had no connection to Maria Torres. She would have thought they'd be all over this job, wanting in on the action.

"Because Jack, Bliss, Connor, and Ava are known to be supporters of Maria's and also Fernandez's biggest vocal opponents. If they came to Vegas and started hunting around, they could send Ortega and his operation to ground. Jack is known to be relentless."

Rissa had discovered Jack's tenacity during the job that reunited Jack and Bliss.

"True." Rissa still didn't get why they'd trust a new prospective employee with such an important job.

"I'm the secret weapon." But he said it with a self-deprecating smile as if he didn't take himself too seriously. "No one knows about me yet."

Rissa wanted to roll her eyes. Yes, he was *so* special. "What don't they know?"

She waited impatiently. He was still smiling about his secret. What didn't *she* know? She was missing something crucial here.

He hesitated one more moment, then said, "Jack is my brother."

Yeah, he knew how to stop a conversation cold.

And he wasn't gonna lie, the whole situation still felt weird. It was the first time he'd admitted aloud to anyone but family—and wasn't that an odd word? Family—that he was related to the Stone siblings. The Stones had not just welcomed him with open arms but they'd yanked him through the door, shoved him into a seat at the table, and handed him a plate of turkey and stuffing, before he could even process that he wasn't all alone in the world.

"You're Jack's brother? But…how?"

John skimmed his gaze up and down BB's gorgeous body, lingering on the swell of her breasts and the curve of her ass. Her cheeks flushed at his lazy perusal. He couldn't resist needling her just a little. Maybe as payback for her less-than-accommodating attitude earlier. "I'd think a woman as shit hot as you would know about a baby daddy."

She thunked her head into her hand. "You know what I mean."

"Half-brother."

"Another one?" She burst out before her eyes rounded as she realized how inappropriate her comment was.

"Yeah. Daddy dearest is a complete dog."

John had yet to meet his father. He wasn't too keen on it. He'd been pissed after his mother's revelation. As he discovered more about his sperm donor, meeting the man had dropped to the bottom of his priorities. But in searching for his father, he'd found half-siblings galore.

And that was a serious bonus. Oddly, though he hadn't been searching for them, he was starting to like the fact that he had a group of people who had his back.

Her mouth rounded in a plump O. Her lips were slicked in all-American flag red. A color of power and patriotism. All control and attitude.

Fuck him. He tried to stop his thoughts from going to sex. But it was difficult. He hadn't had sex in forever. Right now he was hard enough that he felt like his dick would crack off if he even moved. Marissa Evans, *Rissa* he corrected, was smoking hot. Perfection in female form. She was so out of his league, she was in another stratosphere.

Not to mention almost a complete bitch.

Almost.

There were glimpses now and then of a softer, sweeter woman but then the strident witch would come roaring back.

Although it might be worth putting up with the bitch for the sweet surcease of her body. At least once. Maybe several times. Maybe for one night.

About ninety-nine percent of the time, she had balls of steel. But every once in a while he'd catch a glimmer of vulnerability which made him think that the bitchy attitude was actually an act to mask something else.

Usually he went for sweet women. Low maintenance,

easy-going, fun-loving. No drama and no fuss. Until that sweet woman started wanting things he didn't want to give, and then he'd end it. Being in the military, he'd seen enough broken marriages to know that he should steer clear of anything permanent. Being deployed, having to keep secrets, not being able to come home every day. He refused to consign any woman into virtual single motherhood like his mama, or die and leave a woman all alone, again like his mama. Simple, uncomplicated, and short term had been his pattern his entire adult life.

He'd never been tempted.

But suddenly he was out of the military. He wouldn't be gone all the time. He wouldn't have to keep secrets. Or at least no national secrets.

A relationship, a concept he'd sworn off of for so long, was now a possibility. But there was no way in hell this woman would ever go for a washed-out and used-up military man with half a leg. Because, except for her attitude, she was perfection.

She was the embodiment of sexy, sultry beauty. Voluptuous curves, high cheekbones, plump lips, exotically tilted eyes of a striking aquamarine, thick lustrous black hair that swung in a sexy curtain, skimmed her shoulders and framed her smooth, unmarred pale skin.

And he was the polar opposite of perfect. He was a patchwork of scars mostly outside, some inside, mended back together after the IED had ripped his life apart. A messy work in progress, broken but not bowed, flawed but not defeated. He'd worked damn hard to rebound from the destruction, but those scars defined him. Defined who he was, up to this point in his life, and he certainly wasn't going to let her perfection bring him down.

What the hell was he thinking anyway? This wasn't a

date. They were working on a mission that had the potential to send his life in a completely different direction. This week held the promise of regaining a sense of purpose. The last thing he needed was a hookup with her.

John shoved out of the flimsy patio chair. The metal feet screeched across the concrete deck. If he hadn't had his gaze firmly planted on her face he would have missed her slight flinch.

"I'm going to go ice my knee." He patted his swollen knee joint, to remind her, and himself, of his imperfection. The touch emphasized he was the exact opposite of her physical flawlessness, just in case she'd forgotten.

"You want to call Bliss and see if she can come stay with Maria?"

For a few reasons, John, Rissa, and Maria were staying off the Strip at some sort of hotel timeshare place.

One, they thought the noise and chaos of the Strip would be too much for Maria. Jack sure as hell been right on that point.

And two, they wanted to be physically distant from the Stone family.

The idea was to be covert while they were investigating this potential link to the kidnapping from eight years ago. The whole family was coming in town for a wedding. Everyone arrived tomorrow for a pre-wedding family vacation. At the end of the week, Jack and Bliss were tying the knot.

John couldn't be more thrilled for his half-brother. Jack and Bliss seemed idyllically happy.

Although he wasn't sure, John thought the collaboration between him and Rissa was a test drive for partnering with Adams-Larsen on more jobs. Perhaps he would learn what her company's real work entailed. Because on the surface there didn't seem to be much crossover between a humanitarian aid company and an image consulting firm.

One thing he'd learned about Jack, he didn't do anything without thinking through the consequences and results. So if Jack thought partnering with Adams-Larsen was a good idea, then he had his reasons and it was going to happen.

Which meant John couldn't fuck it up by having sex with his temporary teammate. No matter how much his dick wanted it.

When alternate housing for him, Rissa, and Maria was proposed, he'd been happy to carve out a little distance from the rest of the Stone family. He still wasn't completely comfortable when they were all in one place. His four siblings, Jack, Riley, Connor, and Jess, plus their assorted significant others, and Shelley as a surrogate mother, could be a little overwhelming.

However, he was starting to seriously question his sanity in agreeing to share this suite with Maria and the BB. He'd thought it would be plenty big enough for their little team. After all, he'd lived in barracks at Camp Leatherneck. This suite was a fucking palace compared to those living quarters. But that was before he'd become crazy and inadvisably attracted to Rissa Evans.

His stump was hurting. John limped back and forth to the ice machine down the hall. Fortunately the kitchen was stocked with a large soup pot so he brought that and the ubiquitous ice bucket with him. It was still going to take a ton of trips to get enough ice for his ice bath.

He dumped the ice in the giant Jacuzzi tub which was in a nook open to the master bedroom and separated only by a half wall. He'd been given the room with the king-size bed and the larger separate bathroom so that Maria and Rissa could have the room with two beds. Maria was still considered a bit of a flight risk. She'd gotten better in the past six months, more comfortable being around people, but she still had trouble trusting anyone but herself. Which of course was not a surprise.

BB appeared in the kitchen with their ice bucket. "You want help?"

If she'd been perky or condescending, he probably would have brushed her off but after her grudging offer, he surprised himself by answering, "Yeah. Sure."

They walked to the ice machine in silence. The lack of conversation was easy, until it wasn't. A strained quiet filled their awkward trips back and forth from the ice machine to his room. The first time she walked into his bedroom, she stopped cold. "Wow. Nice tub."

She eyed the deep bowl with a multitude of jets and big enough for two. John had a visceral and physical reaction to her appreciation. He pictured her naked, wet and glistening, as bubbles frothed around her showgirl-worthy, truly magnificent breasts. He got lost in wondering what color her nipples were and then wondering what she would taste like.

The violent reaction to the images bombarding his brain was so intense, heat rose between them. And his semi, which he'd sported most of the day, stiffened into a good little soldier. Ready to show her how nice the tub was and how nice he could do her.

He so needed to get laid.

Then he remembered he was missing half his leg. Yeah. So not happening. At least not with her.

She awkwardly turned toward the Jacuzzi and dumped the ice in the slowly filling bowl.

"So how'd it happen?" She was angled away from him as if she didn't want to gawk.

"What?" John was still in a daze from the hot fantasy his brain had conjured as he pictured her naked and willing. His body reacted to the sensual image of sliding into her slick wet heat. Reality struck. He didn't have a chance in hell. She gestured to his leg, still not looking him in the eye. And that was more effective than an ice bath on his erect dick.

"Can't really tell you. It's classified." He said wryly, "However the nutshell, unclassified version, is I got blown up."

"I'm…sorry." Her voice was soft.

Softer than he'd ever heard it, every trace of bitch was gone. But damn if he wanted her fucking pity. Except when she finally gazed at him, those blue-green stunners didn't reflect sympathy. He wasn't sure what was there, but thank Christ it wasn't pity.

"Thank you for your service."

"The civvie contractor next to me wasn't as lucky." John recalled the quiet, civil engineer who'd ended up dead beside him, his body a broken, grotesque skeleton.

And yeah, the loss of his leg was horrible, life changing. But at least he had a life. On his good days he could be philosophical and admit his injury was just a cost of doing war.

Sure, he had bad days where the depression and the "why me?" got to him. But when his brain started to spiral that way he tried to remember that contractor's lifeless eyes and be thankful for his survival. The loss of his leg was a serious blow in many ways but he was one of the lucky ones whose prosthetic options were varied and worked. "So I count my blessings."

She placed her hand on his forearm. The contact sizzled up his arm and down his body. And his wilted erection banged right back into place. John deliberately stared down at her smooth fingers, with those no-nonsense practical nails, wrapped around his arm. Lust flared sharp and sudden in his belly. He tilted his head at an angle to hide his gaze and wondered if she was sending him an unspoken message.

She uncurled her fingers and took a big step back. "I'm…glad you're okay."

That instinctive move away from him told John everything he needed to know. With that one scotch freeing his tongue, he couldn't help but push. "Not glad enough to help me with my problem though, right, BB?"

"Problem?" But her gaze drifted to his crotch and sure enough, her eyes widened at the boner throbbing against his zipper. Instead of running away, she licked her plump red lips. The temperature in the room shot up about a hundred degrees. Her face flushed and her nipples hardened into tight little peaks that pushed against her thin cotton blouse and told him she was as turned on as he was.

Dammit, he ached.

Rissa swayed toward him. But then a sound from the other room hit both their ears as a pot banged on the stovetop. Maria was awake and apparently in the kitchen. Saved from a mission-altering mistake by their team member.

"I'll just…go check on her," BB said. Her voice came out in a breathy rasp, and he wondered if that's what she'd sound like in the middle of sex. He didn't even think that she realized what she'd done when she cast one last, lingering glance at the erection that still hadn't gotten the message that he wasn't getting any.

Rissa pivoted on her heel and rushed out of the room as if a band of Afghani insurgents were on her six. That act brought him back to reality. The only people who'd seen his leg were his doctors and nurses. His last girlfriend, and he meant that term loosely, at the time hadn't been able to deal with the recovery period for an amputee when the last thing on his mind had been sex.

So here he sat over a year later with a massive boner and nowhere to put it. And since he'd waited so long to show his mangled leg to a lover, he certainly wasn't going to start with the beautiful Ball Buster.

His ego was pretty healthy but no sense in getting shot down hard by Miss A plus.

He quickly stripped down and removed his prosthetic with a mangled sigh. His injury was transtibial, which meant he still had use of his knee joint. John braced for the frigid water. The relief for the stump and joint would be fantastic. But he was literally going to freeze his ass and balls off.

He slid down into the water. The shock wilted his erection right quick and his balls shriveled into tight little sacs trying like hell to draw up and hide. Nothing like ice water shrinkage to get rid of an unwanted boner.

John groaned at the frigid cold and then tried to focus on the throb of pain in his knee joint rather than the freezing burn everywhere else. He tilted his head back and leaned against the rim of the tub.

John lifted his right leg out of the water and rested it along the edge of the tub and sank his hips farther down. The position was a little awkward, his half leg in the ice, which spread his crotch wide, unfortunately his cock bore the brunt of the cold but it was easier on the rest of his body. He groaned again when the cold finally started to work on the ache in his residual limb.

The door to the bedroom burst open and Rissa barged in to the tub area. "Are you okay?"

She was breathing hard. Her gaze skimmed over him checking for injury or hurt. But as she figured out he was fine, her focus lingered on his abs before dropping to his dick.

He was so stunned he didn't even bother to cover his now less-than-impressive package.

Amazingly, his cock responded anyway as he took in her partially unbuttoned blouse and the tantalizing peek of blue lace. Even with the extremely cold water, he started sporting wood. Fantastic. He needed to get her the hell out.

Was he okay? "Why wouldn't I be?" He ignored the deep pounding of his heart, the beats echoed loudly in the pulse of his erection.

She continued to stare as she squeaked out a breathy, "Oh."

Then as if she finally registered his state and the fact that she'd burst in on him naked, she started babbling. "Oh my God. I'm sorry! I didn't…." She whirled around so that her back was to him. "I thought you were…."

"Thought I was what?" He really did want to know because he'd seen the distress on her face when she'd barged in. Somewhere in the back of his mind he registered that he'd finally found something that could fluster the innate cool confidence she exuded.

"I heard you groan and thought maybe you were hurt." Her head tilted back and she murmured at the ceiling. "Fuck."

Hell yes. Let's do it. He could be out of the tub and at the bed in a matter of seconds. But now that she was facing away from him and was embarrassed, he became conscious of the fact that he was naked.

And she'd been worried that he was hurt.

"Just because I'm missing part of my leg doesn't make

me incapable of—" anything except continuing to be a Marine, "—taking care of myself."

Her lack of faith in his competence crushed his erection faster than the damn freezing water.

Her back stiffened and her neck went tight. "That's not what I meant," she said harshly.

She'd seen his stump. Not even with the silicone sock on. Right out there, all red and scarred and below the joint just…gone.

A sick miasma welled up inside him. Even if she'd been contemplating sex earlier, he was pretty sure neither of them would survive the reality of his ugly swollen stump and hideous scars touching her flawless perfection.

And yeah, he hadn't really considered the logistics of sex either. Unless he was on the bottom, his ability to move would be limited. At least until he got the hang of having only one foot.

The scars were still red and angry. The VA doctors assured him that over time they would fade. He was vain enough that he massaged both shea butter and emu oil on his stump every night. But the IED that had taken his lower leg had also left jagged scars where the shrapnel ripped through his quads and burned his skin.

He wasn't about to show her weakness by letting on how disturbed he was that she'd seen his scarred stump. His disfigurement was like a train wreck. You were unable to stop staring.

"Well, gawk your fill at the hideous, disfigured mess that used to be my leg." John hoped his taunt would get her to leave. That she wouldn't take him up on the challenge. He willed her to run away. "Get it out."

To his utter and complete surprise, and fucking mortification, she did turn around. He had his arms propped up on the sides of the tub, fists clenched, biceps bulging, because what the hell? But he'd asked for it.

He wasn't about to show her how much he cared if she inspected his leg, his scars. He hated feeling vulnerable. But fuck if he'd let her know.

Her gaze skimmed over his chest and abs, then stopped on his groin, and miraculously he started to get a stiffy. Then her curious gaze finally slid to the hideous reality of his stump.

"Does it hurt?"

He resisted the urge to cross his hands over his dick, cover up and hide. "Every damn day."

She lifted her gaze to his. Something in there made him pause. Because he didn't see pity. Or disgust. Or horror. He saw empathy. Understanding. And that sense that her bitchiness was hiding something came back full force.

In that moment, a connection forged between them. A bond, a thin skein of awareness unfurled and reached between them, like a vine twisting around them, twining them together in unity, solidarity.

"Not everyone's scars are visible," she murmured. Then she walked out, closing the bedroom door very, very quietly.

And he wondered…what the hell just happened?

HOLY MARY MOTHER OF GOD.

Rissa stepped back into the living room area and tried to get her heart rate to settle. She had never had such an intense physical reaction to a man. His body was a work of art. The single band of tattooed flowers around his left biceps, the hard planes of his chest, the rippled eight pack, and strong muscular thighs dusted with dark hair.

A nest of darker black curls cradled his cock, which based on the frigidity of that water should have been the size of a pencil, instead the thick stalk that lay against his groin was impressive.

She swallowed, her throat parched, and envisioned his cock fully erect. The picture caused her breath to catch as she imagined the pleasure of taking him in her mouth. Her nipples ached and her core primed. Damn, it had been way too long since she'd had sex. And now she wanted....

Oh, bad, bad idea, Rissa.

She might not be damaged on the outside like John but she was clearly the more messed up mentally. She'd nearly jumped out of her skin on the balcony when his chair screeched against the cement.

Rissa had been battling her internal demons for over two years. And they pretty much hadn't gotten any better. She was a fucking basket case. Her memories rose up at odd times and punched her in the gut. Rissa had to keep her focus on the job.

The insane, off-the-hook attraction that sizzled between her and John was off-limits.

No, the lust was not one sided.

Even if it had been a while since she'd seen a penis up close and personal, she knew that water that ice cold should have rendered him completely flaccid but he'd been aroused. As if their bodies were in complete and utter synchronicity, their pheromones demanded satisfaction, overruling their brains.

She couldn't afford to be distracted by the totally swoonworthy former Marine. She needed to get her head firmly back on the mission. She was as jumpy as a kid home alone, watching a scary movie. If she was this jittery she could only imagine how Maria was feeling. Admiration for all that the younger woman had endured and overcome would sneak up and hit Rissa at odd times.

Maria, and her friends, deserved nothing less than Rissa's full effort.

"Everything okay?" Maria stood in the small but functional kitchen, her hands linked in prayer position. Her fingers were red, and if Rissa wasn't mistaken she'd been twisting them. Worry darkened Maria's striking eyes and her thick lustrous ebony hair curved around her smooth unblemished cheeks.

"Yes." Rissa wanted to put her hand on Maria's shoulder. Give her some comfort but she knew the woman was still hesitant about being touched by people. Instead she gave the woman her most confident smile. "My mistake. He's fine."

Maria's shoulders relaxed. "Good."

Rissa felt compelled reiterate to Maria. "You know you don't have to be here."

"They need to pay," Maria said fiercely.

Rissa had nothing but the utmost respect for this woman. She'd survived years of captivity, trapped in the basement of an abandoned house, her only contact with the outside world a weekly grocery delivery.

Maria had rescued herself. Escaped, and then committed to taking down the man responsible for her kidnapping. Unfortunately in this story, Maria was the lucky one.

But now they had a lead on the two missing girls.

They might have been absorbed into a trafficking network. They might be working girls. Might. Might. Might. So many unknowns.

What they did know? José Fernandez had become a champion of the migrant community.

His crusade had brought attention to the disparities between what happened when girls of color were kidnapped versus white children.

And it had all been a lie.

Not the inequality in attention of course but everything else he'd basically engineered to further his own cause. He'd sputtered and denied the horror of that crime when they'd accused him of selling the girls. He was a man of honor. He hadn't taken a dime.

Rissa wanted to howl in frustration. As if not taking any money had made it acceptable. He'd taken only their freedom, their choice, and their futures.

The only way Sophia and Graciela would get back the rest of their lives was if Rissa and John could find them, and save them. She hadn't been able to save her partner. The thought that she could be a savior twisted her stomach. Because this was one mission she couldn't afford to fail.

"We will do everything we can to make it happen," Rissa said.

Maria glanced at the closed door to John's room. Her face was a blank mask and Rissa wondered what Maria was thinking.

"I need—" Maria stopped, swallowed. "I *need* to find them. Help them." The expression on her face was fierce. "No one deserves what happened to us."

"You know it will take time." She didn't want to give Maria false hope. And she also didn't want to lie and tell her everything was going to be hunky-dory if—when—they found the girls. Because they'd been gone for eight years. Rissa shuddered.

Rissa let shame roll through her. Of course Maria knew. Her ordeal hadn't been a piece of cake. A sudden thought struck Rissa. "What about after?"

"After what?"

Maria had spent the past eight years working toward escape. "What did you think about the future after you escaped?"

Maria shrugged.

"You didn't dream of anything?" Rissa knew what her dreams were. She wanted to get back to herself. Get back to the way she was.

"You can't hope." Maria's words were quiet, broken. "It's all about one day at a time."

Rissa couldn't imagine. All she did was live for the future. When she was back. When she wasn't afraid anymore. When her life would return to normal.

Adams-Larsen might be able to help Maria. They had a psychologist on staff who talked to their clients about leaving everything behind. How to look to the future instead of wallowing in the past.

Even though Maria didn't need to disappear, maybe Adams-Larsen could help her transition into her new life.

And the more she examined the idea, the more she loved it. "Think about what you want to do with your life next."

Maria nodded but her vacant glazed eyes told Rissa that she was still just holding on to today. She couldn't yet think about the future.

But she needed to give Maria that. She deserved a future. "You are extraordinary," Rissa said.

"No, I'm not." Maria shook her head, so distressed that Rissa was tempted to back off. Except she couldn't. Maria deserved nothing less than her best. Nothing less than success.

Rissa and John would give Maria Torres her future. She deserved it.

She wanted to tell her so but Maria hadn't had a lot of

experience trusting people. Rissa knew she trusted Jack and Bliss, and Connor and Ava. Sort of. But that was about it.

"I know you don't know me."

Maria's hands fluttered before resting at her sides. As if she wanted to draw as little attention to herself as possible.

"But I see you." In her own way, Rissa was as lost as Maria. She just hid it better.

That's where she needed to keep her head. Protecting Maria Torres. Finding the man who'd stolen Maria's friends. Finding her confidence back in the field. She had to put aside her fears to help Maria.

That's what she needed to focus on.

Making things right for Maria. Because she deserved closure. She deserved to look to the future. Rissa would find a way to give Maria hope. To fix Maria Torres's world.

That was what was important. Not the enigmatic, intriguing, compelling man in the other room. Who terrified her on a whole other level.

But she glanced back at the closed door of his bedroom one last time. And wished they were both whole.

CHAPTER 4

John nearly swallowed his tongue.

He sure as hell couldn't speak. Rissa was hotter than summer in Vegas.

Of course, he'd known she was stunning. She had that sexy, sultry style even dressed in mannish pants and a boring button-down shirt. Right now she had on the ultimate little black dress: wide strips of black fabric alternated with strips of black mesh, crossed in a revealing V, highlighting an even more spectacular rack than he'd believed existed earlier beneath that simple white cotton blouse. The concealing and revealing strips let the observer play peek-a-boo with her skin.

Her arms were bare, sleekly toned and lightly tanned, shimmering with some sort of glittery powder. That stunning upper body tapered to her trim waist and down to the generous curve of her hips.

She had curves.

Lots of feminine curves that would be perfect handfuls no matter where he put them, her breasts, her hips, her ass.

He pulled at the cuffs of his tailored suit and stretched

his neck from side to side. Of course he was used to wearing his dress uniform for formal functions, so he wasn't completely out of his element, but he heartily preferred his worn cotton T-shirts and cammies to the tighter, more confining cut of a fancy suit.

"You look…" *hot, sexy, completely out of my league* "…nice," he finished lamely.

She scowled.

Ooookay. Of course, what was he thinking? This wasn't a date.

"You too" was all she said. Then she pivoted sharply, in a maneuver his training instructor would have applauded, toward the door. John mentally sighed. BB was back.

A knock sounded and saved him from shooting off his mouth and saying something snarky. He needed to just suck it up and play nice. Because the more time he spent thinking about this case, the more he grasped that he wanted the opportunity to work with his family.

His sister, Jess, and boyfriend Colin delivered aid to an earthquake ravaged country. Brother, Riley, and Di brought books to the impoverished schools in the Philippines. Jack, Bliss, Connor and Ava, along with Stone Consulting, helped Maria. Now the family was searching for Maria's friends. Even stepmom Shelley was actively involved in the food bank. John wanted to be a part of making a measurable difference in people's lives.

Rissa peered through the peephole and then let out a squee.

She yanked the door open, tugged Bliss Lee into the their suite, and wrapped her in a quick embrace. "Oh my God, it's so good to see you."

His brother Jack followed close behind his fiancée. Bliss's half Asian heritage was evident in the exotic tilt of her green eyes and her half Irish in the burnished auburn of her hair.

"You too." Bliss squeezed her friend tight. Then she held on to Rissa's elbows and leaned back, skimmed over her. "You doing okay?"

John frowned. There was a note of concern in Bliss's voice. It wasn't a general question. What was that about?

Rissa laughed jerkily. "My feet are already killing me," she deflected.

Bliss was concentrating on Rissa like she wanted to say something else.

Jack stole John's attention when he wrapped his arms around his shoulders and clapped him on the back in a typical man hug. "Hey, man."

John cleared his throat. "Hey." Then he backed away.

A large smile wreathed Bliss's face. "John!"

She hustled over and gave him a hug. John stood still in her affectionate embrace, then awkwardly patted her before dropping his hands to his sides. He was still a little uncertain with his siblings' partners. Not that they'd made him feel anything but welcome, but still the physical affection they tended to bestow on him was disconcerting.

"You two ready to hit the club?" Bliss studied them both. "You look good together."

Bliss put her hands on her hips and cocked her head to the right. She stepped up to John and unbuttoned the top two buttons of his blue button-down shirt and pulled the material open. She patted his chest. "Better."

She eyed Rissa. "Riss, that dress is hot."

A flush blossomed over Rissa's bare collarbone, sped up her neck, and edged toward her hairline. "Thanks." She'd tilted her head so that the curtain of her hair hid her eyes for a moment.

John swallowed. He was going to have to concentrate hard at the club and keep his attention on finding the women and not on his companion.

"Maria is in the shower," Rissa said softly. "But she knows you're coming."

John patted the breast pocket of his suit coat. "I've got the age progression photos of Sophia and Graciela."

Jack handed John a wallet with ID and credit cards. "Con got you set up with the cover identities we discussed yesterday. They will withstand a minimal background check and quick Google search tonight. We've got our new tech person working on building a more comprehensive dossier."

Nice. Jack must have had the basics of their cover in place before they'd even arrived in Vegas. There's no way he could have gotten the information integrated into search engines and databases in the few hours since John had called him to let him know that he and Rissa were going to the strip club.

Bliss glanced curiously between the two of them. "What's your cover?"

"We're an adventurous couple on the prowl for a threesome," Rissa said huskily. She had a faint blush on her high shimmering cheekbones. "Preferably Latina."

Bliss sobered. "God, those poor girls. We need to find them."

Everyone nodded.

"Are you armed?" Bliss asked.

John said, "Not this time. Strictly reconnaissance and information gathering."

Rissa was shaking her head vehemently.

"Good," Bliss replied. She wrapped one arm around Rissa's shoulder and squeezed. "You'll do great."

What the hell was that all about?

"J, can I talk to you for a sec." Jack gestured to the slightly offset living room and distracted him.

"Sure." He followed Jack until they were separated enough to have a private conversation. It was then that John noticed the strain around Jack's eyes. Whenever he wondered if he really was related to the Stones all he had to do was look in the mirror. He had the same shape eyes as Jack, Riley, and Jess. "What's up?"

Jack hesitated before shooting a furtive glance at his bride to be. *What was going on?*

"I'm counting on you to handle this while I focus on a few other things."

They'd had a variation of this convo before. He knew about Jack's secret mission. Oddly, John was the only one of their siblings who Jack had confided in. "Yeah. Don't worry. I want justice for Maria. And her friends."

"I can't tell you how much I appreciate this." Jack had retired from the Navy on his own. No disability hovering over his head to force him into making a choice he wasn't ready to make.

John had worked through the rage and injustice of his injury after months of therapy. "It's not like I'm not getting something out of it too. I'm grateful for the opportunity to do something worthwhile."

It might not be saving entire villages. Or keeping his country safe. But at least he had the chance to save women who didn't deserve what happened to them.

Jack was silent for a moment. "I'm really glad you decided to ring our doorbell."

John wanted to break the fraught moment but his throat was crowded with the same emotion shining from Jack's eyes. And it was hella uncomfortable. He was a guy. A guy used to not sharing his emotions. Thankfully, Jack switched subjects.

"Shelley is getting some odd attention," Jack finally said, rubbing the white scar that bisected his thick eyebrow with his thumb.

John didn't know Jess's mom well but she had made him feel instantly at home at her house in Monterey. "What kind?"

"Stalker-ish." Jack frowned. "My buddy Ric is keeping an eye on her."

John wasn't sure why that made Jack scowl but before he could ask, Jack continued, "I'm already split in a few different directions. But if you need me, I'm there for you."

If Jack was truly interested in having John come to work with them, he needed to know that John could think and plan on his own.

"We can handle it." At least for now. It would be arrogant to assume that if they found the girls that they wouldn't need help to rescue them. But until they located Sophia and Graciela, they had to focus on the smaller goal.

"Good." Jack narrowed his eyes. "Con is monitoring your cover identities. But I've also got him working on Shelley's problem."

John raised his eyebrows. "Okay."

"I believe in you. But I want you to keep me in the loop." Jack rubbed his hands over his face. "And protect our girl Rissa."

Protect her?

"She hasn't been in the field in a while." Jack pursed his lips as if he wanted to say more. Fuck, what was going on? Was he being set up to fail?

Then remorse spread through him. Jack wouldn't do

that to him. He had to trust his brother to have his back if needed.

Relief, pride, and determination spiraled through him before he finally replied, "You got it."

Bliss chose that moment to saunter over to where they stood. "Usually it's the girls whispering on the sofa." An indulgent amusement sparkled in her emerald eyes.

"I've got an errand to run." Jack brushed his fingers through Bliss's red hair and tucked a strand behind her ear.

"Oh." Her lips stretched over her teeth, more forced now, and the sparkle was gone as she glanced between the two of them.

"Sorry, babe." Jack pressed a kiss to her temple. "I'll be back a little later."

"It's all good." In the last moments Bliss's shoulders tightened.

Jack did appear to be sorry. John hoped he knew what he was doing.

"Nice to see you, Rissa." Jack smiled and sauntered out the door before anyone could say a word. He scattered almost as if he didn't want to be alone with Bliss before John and Rissa headed out.

Once Jack was gone, Rissa's anxiety seemed to ramp.

"You should get going." Bliss nudged them toward the door, seeming more distant and sad as they said goodbye. "This is important. Let's bring those girls home."

THEY'D MADE it past the velvet rope and a bouncer who looked like he could bench press a small stretch limo. The interior of the upscale club was decorated in retro Vegas glitz. Heavy bronze velvet curtains hung on the walls. Small round tables lining the stage and scattered throughout the floor were decorated with a single fake votive candle. Ornate Art Deco bronze sconces in the shape of women's breasts, set along the walls between the velvet curtains, flared muted yellow lighting. Teardrop chandeliers with tiers of crystals hung over the long copper-and-bronze bar along the far wall.

With spotlights covering most of the runway, the occupants' focus would naturally be drawn to the stage and the entertainment.

Provocatively attired cocktail waitresses efficiently worked the room, clad in black satin bustiers cut high on their hips, underwire cupping their breasts and their nipples showing through the sheer black mesh. Thigh high fishnet tights and silver patent leather pumps with six inch heels emphasized their legs. Their faces were slathered with makeup, lips slicked with gold glossy lipstick. The final touch was a little top hat with a plume of gold-tipped black feathers and a small web of netting to cover their eyes.

Cigarette girls with old-fashioned trays full of cigars, cigarettes, candy, roses, condoms and lube roamed the floor offering their wares. Rissa wondered if that's all they were offering.

Even though this club primarily featured female "dancers," their clientele trended toward couples, so the bartenders were totally ripped guys with tight black pants, naked chests, and tiny little gold bow ties around their thick, chemically enhanced necks.

This place screamed sex. High class, discreet, sex for sale. John placed his hand on the small of Rissa's back, publicly claiming her. The totally innocuous contact sizzled through her veins, and a sensual buzz skimmed along her nerve endings.

She'd been fighting the near visceral attraction to him since they met. But there was no place in this op for her get distracted by their sexual chemistry.

She'd tried before to separate sex from emotion, and the last time it hadn't gone so well. Sex was too intimate. Too revealing. And the last thing she needed was to share her current insecurities with her partner.

Relax, Riss.

His touch and the reason they were in this sleazy, covered-with-a-veneer-of-class-and-shit-tons-of-money strip club had her nerves strung tighter than a trip wire and her stomach on high alert. John led her to a table in a back corner. They would have a view of the stage, the bar, and the hallway that led presumably to the bathrooms. From here Rissa could see a velvet-roped staircase at the end of the hallway.

She sank into the plush booth at the black linen-covered table and scrutinized the interior, trying to project an air of indulgent curiosity, as if perhaps it was her first time in a strip club. It was actually her first time in a strip club this nice. She'd been on a sting a few years back where she'd waitressed in a gentleman's lounge but her outfit had been nowhere as revealing as what these servers were forced to wear.

"Hello, my name is Bunny. I'll be your server tonight." The platinum blonde waitress leaned over their table. The sheer cups of her bustier barely restrained her enormous breasts, and the creamy mounds nearly spilled from her top as she bent nearer to be heard over the piped-in instrumental jazz. "What can I get for you?"

John barely even glanced at the blatant display of flesh before he smiled at Rissa, a look tinged with affection as he wrapped his arm around her shoulders, kind of like Bliss had done earlier to Jack…before he'd ditched her.

Even Rissa had caught the tension between her friend and her fiancé.

"What would you like, honey?" John nuzzled the sensitive spot behind her ear and goose bumps shivered over her bare skin.

Rissa couldn't deny that his complete lack of response over the waitress's attributes sparked a little glow in her heart. "I'll have a gin and tonic." Clear liquid that she'd be able to dump in the planter next to her without anyone noticing. The last thing she needed was alcohol in her system.

Her heart was already pounding like the organ was three sizes too large for her ribcage. And nerves had her fingers trembling and her blood sizzling.

John smiled at her, the curl of his mouth and the crinkle at the corner of his eyes in complete contrast with the assessing look he was throwing her way. He could tell something was wrong.

"Just a soda pop for me." John boomed, "With a chaser of Glenlivet."

John handed the waitress a black Amex card embossed with their cover persona name. When they ran the check on them, they'd find out that John and Marissa Walker of Houston were from old money. Old oil family. With lots of cash and very little in the way of pesky morals. According to Jack, Con had been developing the background dossier on the Walkers for a while.

If Ortega's organization dug deep, they would find some more salacious stories about the Walkers. Charges dismissed. Rumors of less-than-savory acts. Just enough sketchiness that they might be able to weasel in without suspicion.

The waitress straightened back up and thrust her breasts forward. "I'll be right back." She sauntered toward the bar, her ass cheeks half bared by the bottom of the bustier. Every single strut of her patent-leather-clad feet conveyed serious annoyance.

Rissa fought the urge to giggle. The waitress was deeply put out that John hadn't bowed to the glory of her breasts. She propped her arms on the table and whispered in his ear, "She's not very happy with you." The urge to tease bubbled up, overcoming her other worries. She'd had real dates that were less attentive than John Pulaski.

John curled his fingers around her left hand. Rissa's breath caught at the casual touch. Air stuttered in her lungs as he lifted her fingers to his lips and placed a lingering kiss on the very tips of her fingers. It should have been a silly gesture. A manufactured attempt at pretend intimacy. Instead, her whole body came to life and the light contact sizzled along her nerve endings.

"Yeah. Wonder why?"

She started to explain the concepts of reciprocal attraction but then he brushed his nose along the inside of her wrist and all her thoughts fled.

Dammit she couldn't concentrate.

"What are you doing?" Her voice came out wispy and breathless, sounding nothing like the rough, tough, street-smart FBI agent she used to be. Her face was close to his, the penetrating pierce of his hazel gaze seemed to melt her into a puddle of gooey arousal.

"Lavishing my wife with attention."

Her heart clenched at the word *wife*. It had rolled so easily off his tongue. And he was enjoying the intimate public contact. Heat rose from his body, the scent of his soap or cologne, a brisk evergreen, teased her senses.

"You ever been married?"

John was so close, she could see the specks of gold in his eyes, and the deep thick fringe of his darker brown lashes. "Nope. Wouldn't do it when I was active duty."

His thigh pressed against hers, the heat from his body was like an inferno. He curled one forearm with hers and continued to press nipping kisses along her knuckles. God, she could barely concentrate. They were supposed to be casing this strip club, studying for something, anything that might indicate that trafficked girls ended up here. So far, their waitress and the cigarette girls were not putting off any frightened or coerced vibes. Of course, she couldn't always tell but she used to have pretty good instincts. So instead of concentrating on the employees, she might as well work on cementing their cover.

So no ex-wife. "How's your girlfriend feel about you living with another woman for a few weeks?"

"No girlfriend either." His eyebrows raised inquisitively.

The sense of relief at his admission took her off guard. She was way too happy about it. But he was big, handsome, heroic. No way he wasn't in high demand. "What happened?"

He blinked, his gaze shielded from hers, but the playful quirk of his mouth was gone. Oh, he was still smiling but his lips were tight, stiff. "She couldn't deal with my leg."

Rissa lifted her other hand to his face, rubbed the burgeoning stubble on his chin. "What a bitch." She smiled as if she'd just whispered something naughty to him, keeping her smile light, seductive. But inside, she wanted to growl and frown.

John snorted. "Can you blame her?" With his nose, he traced the shell of her ear.

She backed away from him so that he could see her face.

"Yes," she said fiercely breaking character for a moment. No way as she going to let that derisive, dismissive comment pass.

They were isolated, encompassed by the dark shadows surrounding their table, wrapping them in an intimate embrace as if they were the only two people in the joint. He hadn't shaved, leaving a dark shadow of scruff that dusted his jaw and framed his mouth. His beard was tingly against her palm, and a new subtle tension wound between them as he nuzzled her skin with his mouth.

The press of his lips against the soft sensitive flesh of her bare palm zapped a bolt of arousal straight to her girl parts.

His girlfriend had definitely been a fool.

The wonder in his eyes was a revelation.

As their waitress dropped Rissa's drink between them, the thunk of solid glass against the linen tablecloth echoed like a shot.

Rissa jerked at the noise, then pulled away from the mesmerizing spell of his gaze to see her G & T on the table, some of the liquid dribbled down the side as the drink sloshed in the glass.

Rissa zoomed her gaze to the waitress, who smiled snottily and then placed John's coke and Glenlivet gently on the tabletop in front of him.

"How long until the entertainment starts, darlin'?" He laid the Texas accent on thick.

"Any minute, cowboy." She eyed John like a woman on a diet who hadn't had any carbs in twenty-one days. "Anything else I can get you?" she purred.

John glanced at Rissa, and she knew she wasn't going to like whatever came out of his mouth next. He made a little come-hither motion to the waitress with his index finger. For a few moments she'd forgotten this wasn't just a date. She'd forgotten that their intimacy was just a cover for finding out what was going on behind the glitz and glamour at this place.

Until her "husband" flirted with their waitress.

She leaned so close that John, and Rissa, had a clear view of her cleavage beneath her bustier.

"If the missus and I were interested in a little…" John paused expectantly, his gaze skimming through the quickly filling main room of the club since the first show of the night was about to start "…companionship. Do you have an idea where we might find a willing lady?"

She stood up slowly, assessing them with a tight smile and a small frown between her dark-dyed brows. "I'm sorry, sir. I wouldn't know of anything like that here." But her gaze shot to the roped-off stairway and Rissa knew she was lying. Could be they were cautious here. Prostitution in Clark County was illegal. But it was an open secret that Sin City was crawling with sex-for-hire workers. One would assume the waitress would get a cut, or a finder's fee, if she referred a customer to services offered. "This is a legal club."

"I kindly appreciate that. Well just in case something comes to your recollection, we're partial to our brown sisters to the south." Trying to push her in the direction of a Latina woman. The exact opposite of the Marilyn Monroe lookalike waiting on their table. No wonder the girl was pissed.

Rissa couldn't help but be amused at her frustration. She'd bet the woman didn't get rejected often.

Bunny nodded tightly. "Can I get you anything else before the show starts?"

"Keep the drinks coming," John ordered with a smarmy smile. "I've got a large…appetite."

Once the waitress stepped away from the table, John lifted his whiskey and downed it in one gulp.

"We're supposed to be working," she hissed. They needed to be at full operating potential. And John didn't know it but Rissa was already working at a disadvantage.

Her gin and tonic might take the edge off her tension but Rissa didn't want anything to impair her judgment or reaction time.

"This is just exploratory." John smiled tightly. Only Rissa could see the tension in his shoulders. She had the strangest urge to rub his shoulders and along his back, to ease the discomfort she sensed. "She was watching. Don't worry. I'll dump the next one."

Rissa lifted her glass languidly, tilted her head, and pretended to flirt with her fake husband. "Cheers."

He clinked his glass against hers and lifted the glass of coke to his lips.

Rissa took a healthy sip of her G & T and wished that she could indulge just a little more. But the truth was that for her first time back in the field, the last thing she needed was liquor. She purposefully relaxed her shoulders and kept her expression light.

For the next twenty minutes, John fake downed his scotch and Rissa dumped her gin in the plant next to her. The waitress had continued to flirt with John and ignore Rissa. Bunny, yeah, she'd bet that wasn't her real name, had been very friendly.

John kept his banter playful but not too suggestive, without leading her on, as Bunny served them round three.

The music indicated the show was about to start.

John slung his arm over Rissa's shoulder and shielded her from the wait staff. He nuzzled her ear. She tried to ignore the rush of pleasure at his touch. "Now would be a good time to dump the drink." She tilted the glass so that most of it poured out and into the potted plant behind her chair.

"Nice." He admired her handiwork, never taking his gaze from the stage. John's fingers toyed with her hair, the small gesture far more intimate than the arm around her shoulders, bringing home the fact that it had been a long fucking time since she'd had sex.

Right after the incident, she'd been on administrative leave with pay while the Office of Professional Responsibility reviewed the postmortem on the tragically failed op and her role in her partner's death. During that awful period, she'd sought comfort and salvation in sex. But every encounter just left her feeling worse. Finally she was cleared, and could have gone back to work. Except…she couldn't go back to the FBI. She couldn't go back to a job that had taken so much.

Thank God, Jillian Larsen had offered her a job, a way to keep busy until she was ready to get back into the field. She'd gone from total promiscuity to total nun-like behavior, not in the headspace where physical interaction, platonic or sexual, was wanted or appreciated. At first she'd been too busy just getting through the work day. She'd basically put her whole life on hold for the past two years.

Until Jill sent her to Las Vegas for this job.

Damn Jill for knowing what Rissa needed before she knew it.

But her boss couldn't possibly have known that Rissa would have such an immediate and intense reaction to John Pulaski. A reaction so strong, her impulse was to back away, hide in the bathroom, until John got the info they were here to gather.

But the Senior Special Agent she used to be, the one that

Jillian had faith in, wouldn't let her back away from what she needed to do.

Rissa placed her hand on his thigh and his entire body tensed. "Relax. I'm just getting a little frisky." Then it occurred to her that he might be worried about her hitting his prosthesis.

John's teeth gleamed with a tight smile. "Don't get too close to the family jewels."

She leaned close and nipped at his jaw. "Cameras, everywhere. We need to play to that." And hope that whoever was watching didn't see them dump their drinks.

Rissa moved her hand closer to his thigh and accidentally brushed against his erection.

"Told ya' darlin'." His smile was far more forced. And Rissa wasn't sure but there might be a bit of flush on his cheekbones.

"Relax." Her smile was determined. "I got this."

The lights dimmed. The music swelled in the intimate venue and Rissa leaned against John.

He smiled tensely as their waitress dropped off more cocktails and removed the empties from their table. "Would you like another soda?" She eyed the nearly full glass.

"This one'll do me for now." John smiled and tilted his head so he could watch the girls on the stage.

The opening number was more of a revue. There were elaborate headdresses and skimpy costumes and glitter dust and thick eyelashes and stiletto heels and nearly bare asses and pasties. But no actual stripping.

Bunny sauntered away, swinging her nearly bare ass, her perfectly rounded white cheeks on display as the stage went dark.

Without warning, loud pops shattered the darkened

venue. Rissa's heart exploded in her chest. Gunshots! Not again.

She grabbed John and tried to shove him under the table as she dove beneath the protective barrier.

Her heart popped in her chest like the bang of an AR15 on full auto. So fast, her breath trapped in her lungs, terror froze her, and she was about to start hyperventilating.

Acrid smoke burned her nostrils as she gasped for clean air.

Not again. Not again. That thought whizzed through her mind like bullets.

John, she had to save John. Her partner. She couldn't let John down. He had to survive. He had to.

She refused to let another partner die.

Fuck.

John's head banged on the edge of the table as he resisted Rissa's attempt to yank him to the floor. What the fuck?

For a second he was off balance. His prosthesis worked well most of the time but he had to maintain a careful center of gravity or he'd over- or under-balance. He managed to press his palm to the banquette seat so that he didn't end up on his ass.

He had a clear view of Rissa under the table as the fireworks popped and banged, lighting up the center of the stage. The smoke from the fog machine didn't obscure the air beneath the tablecloth so he had a clear view of his "wife." Her face was stark with fear and her glassy pale eyes brimmed with unshed tears.

"Not again. Not again," she kept mumbling, still tugging on John's arm.

She was completely losing it. He should be pissed. But her lost, torn expression was breaking his heart. She had gone to another place, one where she had no cognizance of her surroundings. Of who she was, who he was, or what they were doing here. And fuck him but he'd seen this kind of disassociation before.

He had to get through to her. Had to get her back with him and at least partially under control.

They needed to get the fuck out of here. Now.

Before she completely blew their cover.

"Come on." He tugged on her hand. She was still gripping his wrist tightly, her nails digging into his skin with super-strong fear as he gently helped her back onto the seat. As she was righting herself, Bunny strode up to the table. John automatically blocked Rissa from the waitress's sight. He shifted and spoke to Rissa in a low voice.

"I need you to do whatever I tell you, no arguing, no hesitating." John shot Rissa a "shut up and let me get us out of this" stare. She nodded, seemingly ready to follow even if she wasn't completely with it.

"Kiss me," he whispered under his breath and hoped she had enough presence of mind to heed his command. "And sell it."

"Everything okay?" Bunny leaned around John to observe Rissa.

John felt the warm suction of her mouth on his neck and his cock, which still hadn't recovered from her lengthy perusal while he was in the tub, roared back to full attention. God damn, he was going to be walking through this damn place with a club in his pants.

Rissa moaned low in her throat and her tongue was slicking up his neck. Thank Christ she was playing along. But he had to wonder based on her enthusiasm if she'd transferred her fear into desire.

He pasted on his most charming smile, which wasn't all

that charming. "I think my wife is a little…under the weather."

"Under the table," Bunny grumbled.

"Just close out my tab," John commanded as if he'd been born with that silver spoon that was listed on his fake credentials.

Fortunately they were on their fourth cocktail in about forty-five minutes so it was conceivable that she was drunk as a skunk. Rissa's glassy, unfocused gaze and slick mouth only seemed to underscore his statement as she placed little biting nips over his collarbone, supposedly completely oblivious to their audience.

The girls on the stage were still at the beginning of their bump-and-grind show, tearing off little bits of cloth in the American Flag pattern at slow, teasing intervals.

John signed the bill with a flourish and Bunny handed back his black credit card.

"That's for you, darlin'" He tossed a hundred dollar bill on the table and slid out of the booth. Since Rissa had managed to pull out all the sex kitten stops, Bunny likely figured they were about to go at it on their ride home. "Thank you kindly."

"My pleasure," she purred.

He dismissed her. "We'll have to catch the show another night."

"Thank you, sir." Bunny smiled vacuously as she tucked the bill into her cleavage. Then she slid a piece of paper into John's palm and eyed his wife with consideration. "Hope to see you again."

While waiting for the show to start, the swanky club had filled to capacity. John supported Rissa as they wove around the tables and away from the stage. Finally they were at the door and he hustled her out. A line of hopeful people circled around the corner waiting for a chance to get in. Fortunately the show on the stage had enthralled the audience, and the only attention John and Rissa had captured was the assessing scrutiny of the hostess.

He curled his arm around Rissa's shoulders. His palm rubbed against her bare skin of her biceps as he tried to unobtrusively comfort her.

Little tremors rocked her body and her eyes were still dazed and slightly out of focus. He was pretty sure her little freak-out had nothing to do with their objective for the night but until they were somewhere private and could talk he was staying in character.

He nuzzled her neck and let his hands roam over her bare skin.

"We'll be home soon, baby." His voice was far huskier than he'd anticipated. That would work for their cover. But damn he was going to have to take another ice bath to combat the unintended effects of her warm mouth on his skin.

And fuck him, it had been a long time.

They grabbed a taxi from the line outside the club rather than wait for the limo service Jack had put at their disposal. She didn't say a word the entire trip back to the hotel. They couldn't afford to drop out of character until the door closed behind them in their hotel room. If this ring was as high end as they thought, they had the money and the resources to have a pipeline to all sorts of information.

Las Vegas still hadn't recovered from the recession a few years ago.

The taxi drivers were hit especially hard as Vegas was filling hotel rooms with families and couples on vacation. They'd lost a significant amount of corporate business when the trade shows quit coming. Those hefty sales expense accounts were the bread and butter of the taxi drivers. They'd be happy to pick up a few extra bucks supplying business owners, legitimate or otherwise, with information about their fares.

John pulled Rissa on to his lap and kissed his way across the swell of her chest.

She curled her fingers into his non-regulation-length hair and tilted her head back. Even if she wasn't quite with it, she instinctively stayed in character.

He tasted the essence of her. Rissa's skin was exquisitely velvety and smooth. The floral feminine scent that rose from the valley of her cleavage touched off something deep and primal within him. John groaned low in his throat. "Goddamn, you smell fantastic."

Her hip rested against the fucking pipe in his pants. He hoped she wasn't going to go off on him about inappropriate responses once they were back in the hotel room. But besides the small hesitation when she slid against his hard-on, she hadn't reacted at all.

If anything, she seemed lost in the moment.

A restless tension seethed within him. What the hell had happened back there? One minute they'd been watching the show, the next she'd gone completely over the edge. But he wouldn't start yelling until he got her side of the story first.

He kept hearing her whisper "*Not again.*"

As he held her against him, paper rustled in his breast pocket. Bunny had passed him something right before they left. He couldn't retrieve it now with an armful of Rissa but hopefully it was a solid lead.

At the hotel, John swiped his card over the sensor in the elevator, then leaned against the wall and stared at her. Her face was devoid of any expression, except that wasn't quite right. And her aquamarine eyes were unfocused as if she were reliving some other event. Her body was tense as if she was trying desperately to keep that non-expression.

He wanted answers.

The fragility of her features filled him with remorse. Two conflicting feelings simmered inside him. He was trying to reserve judgment until he figured out exactly what had happened at the strip club.

And he still wanted to wait until they were in their rooms.

Finally they were through the door of the suite. Bliss shot off the couch. "You're back early." Then she really examined Rissa and within seconds she had her arms wrapped around the other woman. "What happened?"

John got the message immediately. Bliss wasn't completely surprised that something had gone wrong. Which meant something else was going on here. Something that he had clearly been kept in the dark about. Teammates didn't keep things from each other. That was how people got dead.

"I don't know." John stomped to the sofa. "Why don't you ask *her*?"

Rissa bent her head, her shoulders slumped, arms clasped over her waist. She said, "I freaked out."

Bliss's green gaze shot to John, her eyes wide, concerned. "For no reason?"

"Fireworks. Of course, I didn't know that at first." Rissa tilted her head back. Her wavy black hair tumbled down her back, accenting all that bare supple skin. "Shit. I'm done," she whispered.

The temptation to lay into her was strong but he held off, finally realizing that as frustrated and annoyed as he was, she was beating herself up far more than he could. He still needed to know what the hell happened. What set her off, so they could avoid it or at least prepare for it next time.

Next time.

He already accepted that they'd go out again. They were going to have to in order to follow the lead from Bunny.

"Oh, Riss." Bliss hugged Rissa tightly. "Minor setback."

"You have a lot more faith in me than I do." Rissa smiled wistfully. "Go on home to Jack."

"You sure?" Some emotion that John couldn't decipher flashed across the features of his soon-to-be sister-in-law—or whatever they would be. But it wasn't anticipation. He sure hoped Jack knew what he was doing. Secrets never ended well.

Which led him to his current dilemma. No one was coughing up an explanation regarding Rissa's little breakdown.

He studied her wrapped in that sinful dress, but now he didn't see her hot body or sexy sensual beauty. He was struck by the vulnerability in her eyes.

"Would someone like to tell me what's going on?" John kept his voice low, not wanting to wake Maria and possibly upset her, but he would really like to know what the fuck happened in that club.

Rissa flinched.

Yeah. This was going to be a fun conversation. Sigh.

Especially since Bliss Lee wasn't necessarily surprised that Rissa had freaked out. Which meant that Rissa and Bliss had known ahead of time that something like this might happen.

"Yes." The sad, lost expression had left Rissa's face. She squared her shoulders and addressed him. "I'll explain in a minute."

Bliss grabbed her purse. "You sure you're okay?"

Rissa nodded.

"Should you leave by yourself?" John asked quickly. The last thing he wanted was friction between himself and Jack because he'd let Bliss go home on her own.

"You're kidding, right?"

John shrugged uncomfortably.

Bliss patted her purse. "You do know that I carry a weapon. I can take care of myself."

"Text Jack and let him know you're leaving." John thought that was a good compromise.

"Like a teenager letting daddy know I'm on my way home." Bliss didn't look happy.

"We're investigating a possible kidnapping and prostitution ring," John said patiently. "While the rest of the world thinks you're here for vacation and a wedding, it's never smart to ignore the criminal element. If the wrong people noted that you were here, you could be in danger. There are eyes everywhere."

"Good point." Bliss smirked. "My own experience aside, I think Jack's rep is enough to keep that criminal element off his back. The last thing they want or need is the wrath of Jack Stone. He's relentless."

John wondered if that was a subtle warning. So far his interactions with Jack had been good. "I know. And if anything happened to you on my watch, I'd be history," he said grimly.

"John." Bliss's voice softened. "I didn't mean…."

John forced a grin, baring his teeth in a parody of a smile. "Relax. I know you didn't."

His request worked and she relented. "Fine. I'll text him."

"Thank you." Thank God he hadn't had to force the issue and she'd agreed on her own.

Rissa had just observed mutely as he and Bliss had negotiated.

Bliss said, "I'm off." For a moment, John thought she might say something else. But after one more concerned glance at Rissa, she quietly let herself out of the hotel room.

The silence in the common area of the suite was difficult at best.

John didn't want to interrogate Rissa but he needed to know what he was working with. He couldn't control the outcome, couldn't control the mission, if he was working blind.

John rubbed the back of his neck. His tension headache throbbed right along with his joint. He'd twisted awkwardly when she'd tried to pull him under the table. Even though with his suction assembly the prosthetic wouldn't come off, the tug had bent his knee in an awkward angle.

He had a lot riding on his performance during this operation. He couldn't afford for her to fuck it up.

Fuck. Forget about him. The bottom line was they needed to try to find those girls. For the girls, for the community, for Maria.

All Rissa's attitude was gone. Seeing her slumped, nearly broken on the sofa, loosened an odd wish. He wanted that sass back.

She was stunning, whether as the tough-as-nails ball buster or the slightly defeated woman in front of him.

However, if he showed her any compassion she might break, rather than rise back into the ball buster she'd been for the past two days. So he put aside his compulsion to treat her with kid gloves and growled like the beast he was, "Pull it together."

"I haven't worked in the field in two years."

What? John straightened.

Incredulity, disbelief slammed into him like a one-two punch.

Two years? But Jack and Bliss had said she worked at Adams-Larsen. "Why?" he barked.

"There was…an incident." Rissa rubbed her fingers along the seam of one of the bands of her dress. The stretchy black material had ridden higher on her thighs. The shadowed valley between them promised heaven.

Focus. Idiot.

Fuck.

Her voice was bleak as she relayed the details. A sting gone bad. An op compromised. An agent lost.

"I was placed on disciplinary leave immediately." She avoided his gaze. And even without the compassion, the confident, bitchy woman was gone. "There was an investigation. I was cleared," she said fiercely.

"I thought you worked with Bliss at Adams-Larsen?"

"I do." Rissa laughed bitterly. "I'm the goddamn receptionist."

She answered phones? Then what was she doing working on such an important assignment?

"So, what are you telling me?"

"I haven't been able to go in the field since the shooting," Rissa replied darkly. Her normally incandescent aquamarine eyes were dark with shadows and regret.

"This is your first time out?"

"Jillian thought this assignment would be perfect. Low possibility of violence. This is supposed to be mainly investigative rather than operation based."

Her face was a picture of anguish, her eyes glittering with disappointment but not sadness. Damn, he'd almost prefer she start crying. Ball Buster was gone. In her place was this broken, lost woman. He hated it.

"I'll get out tomorrow. I'm sure Jill can get someone else out here." Her face was hidden by the fall of her hair as she picked at a piece of lint on the black dress.

He was surprised at his immediate, violent response. Every cell in his body reacted negatively. "No."

He threaded his fingers through his wrecked hair and fought for control before he started questioning her. When he fisted his hands, the paper the waitress had given him crinkled in his pocket.

Her head came up, eyes wide, those plump red-slicked lips pursed. "What?"

"No can do." John pulled the paper from his pocket. The one that Bunny the waitress had slipped him right before they left. "We've got a lead. They'll be expecting *you*. Not someone else."

John was so fucking grateful to Bunny for giving him an excuse to keep Rissa with him, even when he wasn't sure why he wanted her there. Her fragile beauty aroused his fierce protective beast, but instinctively he knew that showing her mercy, compassion would only break her more. She needed to fight. Fight back and claim her confidence, otherwise she would continue to be a victim. Continue to cower instead of rise above her fear.

John knew if coddled her, if he gave her the slightest bit of sympathy, she'd crumble. So he pissed her off. He talked to her like he talked to his Marine brothers and sisters in a tone that brooked no arguments. "So toughen up."

CHAPTER 6

Rissa's body went rigid. Who the hell did he think he was?

"We've got to move on this while the trail is hot," John continued, ignoring her anger. "And we can't do that if we aren't honest with each other."

The thought of being completely honest with him curdled her stomach. Bile and shame sloshed like an uneasy sea and she suppressed the need to throw up.

"So from now on, I expect you to keep me apprised, to tell me when there is a situation that will impact our mission." His voice was hard. The lines in his face were carved from concrete, flat and stark. Like the walls of the Hoover Dam, unforgiving, and completely unrelenting. "Maria is counting on us."

Rissa's first instinct was to tell him she couldn't do it.

To refuse. To give up. To go home.

But he'd known exactly what button to push. A noise from the bedroom drew her attention. Maria. How could she let the woman down? She'd survived in the face of nearly insurmountable odds. She'd rescued herself. Stayed sane for eight years of captivity and solitary confinement.

Now, instead of reveling in her own freedom, Maria had gone on a crusade to find and rescue her friends who were taken.

Maria had vowed to keep searching and never give up. Rissa had promised to help find the people responsible.

Rissa didn't want to let Jillian Larsen down either.

Even though Maria had never voiced it, there was a hovering fear that the thugs who took her friends could come back from wherever they'd holed up and steal her away again.

Maria needed her faith in people restored.

If Rissa bailed, she'd be sending the message that Maria wasn't worth it. And that was unacceptable. So as much as Rissa wanted to bail. She couldn't.

All that anger and frustration at John's edict disintegrated when she acknowledged that he was right. On several counts. She should never have kept the information from him. She hated him for being right. Her inadequacies laid bare for him to see and judge.

"Shit," she whispered.

"Is that a yes?"

"Yes," she ground out.

"So we're a team." It wasn't a question. But she answered anyway.

"Yes."

"No more secrets," he demanded.

"No more secrets," she confirmed. Even if she did feel like throwing up.

There was a pause. Silent. Heavy. Fraught. She wondered how he'd ever trust her. Even as she promised, no more secrets.

"I've got your back," John finally said.

A strange and unexpected peace flowed over her. He was there to bear her burdens with her. And the tension she'd been carrying since she landed in Las Vegas eased.

She wanted to reciprocate, but she wasn't sure she could. "Thanks," she managed.

John nodded curtly, as if he was as uncomfortable with her awkward hesitance as she was.

One hurdle at a time.

A curious warmth filled her. This big, bad warrior had her back.

"Then let's see what our pal, Bunny, wrote on this receipt."

John smoothed the slip of paper on the coffee table and bent to read the receipt. "It's a web address. And two words."

"What's the address?"

"Backdoor/AdultServices." John frowned at the paper in his hand. "/Hispanic hotties."

She raised her eyebrows. Backdoor. "Really?"

"What is Backdoor?" John asked.

"You familiar with Craigslist?" she asked.

"Sure, people sell couches and tickets and stuff."

"Yeah. Well they also used to sell 'services' on Craigslist. But after a few high-profile criminal cases, Craigslist decided to shut down that division. So all the people who used to advertise for illegal services, i.e. prostitutes, drugs, porn, moved over to Backdoor."

John just shook his head.

"What?"

"Nothing."

But it wasn't nothing. "What?"

"Some days I'm frustrated that this is what I fought for."

Rissa wanted to reach out to him. But she couldn't make herself take that step. Even though the urge to touch him, comfort him burned through her.

"So she gave us a jump-off point." A burgeoning excitement lit his hazel eyes.

Rissa hated to burst his bubble but she knew better than most that entire lives could be hidden behind legitimate fronts. The cornerstone of hiding people was legitimate structures, legal bank accounts, investments and savings accounts that had some small piece of falsehood and obscured the truth about where the person really lived.

"It's a concrete lead," she agreed cautiously.

"Come on." John smiled, his teeth gleamed, and his perfect lips curved with a mischievous grin. "Get a little excited."

"Just because we found this web address doesn't mean the girls we are trying to find are going to be advertising on this site." She couldn't help but want to slow him down. There were so many ways this lead could go south that getting their hopes up was a mistake.

"I know." John paced the small living area. "But damn, I want to find these girls."

His protective side shone through the leashed energy around him.

"I know." She hated to be the bitch. "But they've been gone eight years, John."

Eight years.

Rissa shuddered at the thought. Even if they found these girls, if what they believed had been done to them was true, it would take a long time for them to get any kind of life back. That horrific type of trauma didn't disappear overnight.

She could feel his censure, even though he hadn't said a

word. But he had to be realistic. "Just because she gave us this website also doesn't mean those girls are going to be there."

Her stomach curdled. They were going to have to view the website. Look at the people being exploited. The odds of finding the women on the first try were astronomical. The reality was that for right now they weren't going to be able to do anything about those other women and men, because Sophia and Graciela were the priority right now.

Plus, they needed to find enough evidence on Manuel Ortega who was responsible for their trafficking. Supposedly the top guy. On paper, in the media, he was squeaky clean. His reputation as a philanthropist supporting women's rights was well documented.

John deflected her focus. "What time do you want to go to the range tomorrow?"

She knew what he was trying to do. Badger her into confronting her fears. But what he didn't understand was she didn't know if she could do it. She'd been to the range. The last time she'd tried to fire her weapon, her hands shook so hard, she'd had to put it down without firing a single round. Her inability to steady her hands was a serious liability.

He deserved to know what kind of partner she wasn't.

Two years ago she'd have been right there with him. Two years ago she would have taken point on their mission to the strip club. Now, she couldn't even watch the show without diving under a damn table.

God, she just wanted her confidence back. Sure she could fake it for a while but the truth was that at night in the dark, she wondered if she'd ever recover from the ordeal that had effectively ended her career.

A thick pall of grief and disappointment swirled in her

gut. She hated what that moment had stolen from her. And clearly Jill had been wrong to put her back in the field. She wasn't ready. She might never be ready.

"I can't."

"Yes, you can," John insisted quietly. "We have a lead. We need you mission-ready. I need you to try. You can do it."

She wanted so desperately to believe that was true. That she could fire a weapon again, if need be. But the reality was that she couldn't even fire under non-threat situations. "I haven't been able to fire a weapon in two years."

God the failure was intense, immediate, and pure agony.

She'd missed the adrenaline rush, the power, the noise. It had been almost euphoric. Better than sex. The endorphins that flooded the blood and brain, pumping the heart, getting every neuron firing. Now she couldn't control the frantic beat of her heart, and the adrenaline made her want to blow chow and pass out.

In her peripheral vision, she watched his large scarred palm reach toward her. Finally his hand settled on her shoulder with a heavy comforting clasp.

"You can do it." His voice was harsh as if he willed her to handle this. And she imagined full of pity.

Rissa shrugged off his hand and laughed bitterly. "Why? Because some macho former Marine says it should happen? Or if you insist long enough that it will happen just because you want it to?" If only it were that simple. If wishing would make it so, Rissa would have been okay the first time she'd tried to fire a weapon after the life-changing incident.

She suddenly regretted the urge she'd had to bare her soul to him.

A guy like him would never understand her insecurities

and fears. Rissa stiffened her shoulders and lifted her chin. Screw him.

John had narrowed his hazel eyes. His jaw could be cut from the stone used to make the granite columns at the Bellagio. "My job as your teammate is to make sure the team functions at optimum performance. In order to do that, all team members need to be honest. I don't appreciate being kept in the dark about your issue."

Her emotions were all over the place. On one hand she wanted to curl up in a fetal ball and hide from him. On the other, she had the furious urge to get right in his face and argue. Even though she knew she was in the wrong.

She'd withheld crucial information about her skill set. The tension headache that had been at low throb all evening had bloomed into edges of a migraine.

Rissa dropped down onto the sofa, rubbed her temples tiredly, and changed the subject. "How do we know we can trust this lead?"

"It's the only lead we have right now." John said, "It's not a question of trust, it's a question of access to Ortega. We've got to follow it."

Her brain kicked in to higher gear. "You let Jack know to keep a lookout for any background checks on our cover?"

"Con is already on it." John rubbed his hands together.

"So if there are any nibbles on our fake background, it's a good bet that the club is vetting us. Which could be why she gave us the website. If we make contact, they will already have information about us." Rissa hoped they would find something on the missing girls.

Anticipation rose up. It had been a long time since she'd felt either useful or effective. While running an office and keeping track of details was an important skill that every business needed, it hadn't satisfied the longing in her soul, that need for adventure found in fieldwork. Every job at Adams-Larsen was important. Every client they helped was a check in the win column for every single employee. But she also knew that she was being underutilized.

Jillian Larsen was a saint. Because she had never made Rissa feel like less because she wasn't in the field. Except now Rissa wondered if Jill knew that she'd been having trouble dealing with the desk job, even if she wasn't sure she was ready for the field again.

But she wished that Jill hadn't pushed her out the door on this case, because Maria and her friends deserved justice.

"Yeah," John replied. There was a note in his voice she couldn't quite place.

"What?"

"It feels good to be doing something worthwhile again." It was like he reached in her subconscious and ripped out her thoughts. It did feel good. The sense of camaraderie she'd felt beat at her like the throb of her headache.

John stood abruptly. "You mind?"

She didn't know what he meant until his hands rested on her shoulders. He dug his thumbs into the muscles at the base of her neck and rubbed in long slow strokes. Rissa's head tipped forward until her chin practically rested on her chest. She fought the urge to moan. "That feels…amazing." He had the perfect touch. Not too light but not overly harsh either. "Where did you learn to do that?"

"When I was first at Walter Reed, I suffered from massive headaches," John said. "The concussive blast gave me recurring migraines for the first few months."

John's fingers eased her pain and Rissa nearly moaned as her body went liquid.

"There was an orderly who was able to give me some

relief. And he explained what he was doing so my girlfriend could give me the same massage."

"That still doesn't explain how you know what to do."

"My girlfriend passed on the massage right about the time she passed on me," he confided mockingly. "So I had to learn to explain what I needed to other people."

And then she felt like a complete asshole, for multiple reasons, but most especially for complaining about her current inability to fire her weapon.

She could hear the humor in his voice. The absolute acceptance of the event that had obviously changed his life. "How did you get to this place?"

He didn't even hesitate. He knew exactly what she meant.

Because she'd been a wreck for two years and the anger and rage still haunted her regularly.

"Therapy." John laughed, his chuckle low and mocking. "Great way to strike fear into every soldier's heart. But I didn't really have a choice. Pretty much had two options, accept and move on. Or reject and be miserable. I chose life."

She could learn a lot from him. His inner strength was beautiful while hers was an unwieldy beast full of anger and frustration. "That's so…."

"A hero is an ordinary individual who finds the strength to persevere and endure in spite of overwhelming obstacles. Christopher Reeve said that." His simple acceptance humbled her.

"You are amazing."

"Hardly." He flushed as if uncomfortable with sharing, and stood awkwardly.

But she couldn't let it go. "I can't imagine." She hadn't moved past the tragedy that had taken her partner's life.

Hadn't managed to put anything back together. John had gone through unimaginable tragedy and had clearly moved on without bitterness or regret.

"I wish I had your strength." Instead of being so damn weak.

"How can you admire strength in others and yet not see it in yourself?" John said. She didn't know whether to be thrilled that she managed to hide her insecurity so well, or to be ashamed because he was so open about his faults.

But he was wrong. She wasn't strong. His comments rubbed her already teetering emotions raw. She needed to hide, get away and reset her internal compass before he realized how much on the edge she really was.

"Good night." She stood abruptly. Rissa carefully opened the connecting door to the room she shared with Maria and ran the hell away.

And she was safe.

CHAPTER 7

Damn phantom pain.

John rolled over and stifled a groan. His leg, the calf that wasn't there anymore, ached like a son of a bitch. He'd pushed his body in a few ways it wasn't quite ready for today and now he was paying for it.

Didn't help that besides the residual pain in his missing limb, he had a hard-on that rivaled the steel-girded Eiffel Tower at the Paris.

He'd thought that he and Rissa had been forging a connection when they'd been confessing their secrets earlier. But then she'd abruptly disappeared.

That hint of vulnerability had been a surprise.

After a long pain-filled hour wherein he tried unsuccessfully to go back to sleep while going over the day and how his perception of her had shifted, John gave up. He might as well review the case file, maybe do some research on Backdoor, see if any of the ads jumped out at him. Find a way to locate those girls—women, now.

He needed to send the website info to Connor and get him running facial recognition analysis on the individual women listed on the site. He should have done it earlier after he and Rissa were done talking, but he'd been distracted by her abrupt departure.

He'd grab a glass of scotch and get some work done while he was dealing with insomnia and pain.

Fuck him. The scotch was in the other room.

John grabbed the crutches by the side of his bed. He wasn't going to put his prosthetic on to get a drink. The worn elastic waistband of his basketball shorts sagged low on his hips. Fuck it. He wasn't putting on more clothes either.

He pushed to standing, fitted the crutches under his arms, and headed to the common area of the suite. The glow of the light over the stove was the only illumination in the impersonal living area.

Quietly, he unscrewed the cap of his twenty-one-year aged scotch. That was one tick mark in the pro column about going to work for Jack. He could afford a much nicer brand of alcohol than he used to drink. With a thick glug, he poured a generous serving of the top-shelf single malt into the cheap glass then humped over to the sofa carefully. The very sparse file on this job rested on the fake wood coffee table. John lowered to the plush sofa and rested against the upholstered back, letting his head loll on the edge.

He propped his stump on the coffee table, and pressed his other foot flat on the floor. With a heavy sigh, he took a sip of the smooth, peaty liquor and then braced the glass on his bare stomach while he contemplated the ceiling.

Thoughts, impressions, memories from the past few days whirled in his mind, forming pictures then disintegrating again; like a kaleidoscope, the conflicting images kept changing. But one specific image haunted him, reforming and coalescing in his mind.

Rissa. On the floor. Under the table. The panic and terror on her face in that strip club, alternately illuminated by the flash of fireworks and hidden by the shadows. That sexy body hidden and revealed by wide strips of silky fabric. The dichotomy of her personality fascinated him. Taunted him with vulnerability and confidence by turns. Each glimpse only intrigued him more.

His brain kept returning to the flash of helplessness in her eyes when she'd admitted that she had a problem.

What he should be remembering was her absolute ball-busting attitude.

But instead, he recalled in perfect detail the strips of flesh revealed by the sex-on-a-stick dress she wore and the shadowed valley of her cleavage. Fully dressed, she'd commanded his attention far better than the nearly nude showgirls on the stage.

As if he'd conjured her up, the door between her bedroom and the living area opened quietly. Rissa crept into the room, clearly trying to be stealthy. He sat in the shadows, knowing she was likely awake for the same reasons he was.

Demons. They haunted her too.

He didn't want to disturb her. Of course, that was self-serving. Because he didn't really want to explain why he was sitting here in the dark either.

There was a slim possibility that she'd grab whatever she needed from the kitchen and head back into her room. Hopefully before she saw him skulking in the dark. John couldn't help but track her movements. The glow from the light above the stove cast her in shadows, emphasizing the lush curves of her ass and breasts. John's mouth watered. She tempted him. Like a siren calling to the sailor, the one who couldn't resist, he wanted to swoop in and draw her to him. But in that moment he realized he wasn't just drawn to her body, although it was spectacular. He was also attracted to her strength, to her intensity, to her sheer determination.

While his mind hungered, his body lusted, responding to her proximity. And he wanted. Even as he shifted restlessly, he acknowledged that he couldn't have her.

"Oh," she gasped when she saw him sitting on the sofa. Busted.

"Hey," he gutted out, his voice gravelly with the burn of embarrassment, and he was thankful that she likely couldn't see him very well.

See his stump. Again.

He silently cursed his instinctive need to cover up, to hide from her. Which pissed him off. He shouldn't be ashamed of his injury. He'd served his country. He'd sacrificed to keep people like her safe, and if she couldn't appreciate it, then fuck her.

Whoa.

John shook his head, trying desperately to get rid of that rage-y rant. She'd never once given him any indication she found his stump disgusting. Clearly he still needed to work through some things.

While he'd been fighting with himself, there was a hitch in her step, and he could almost feel her indecision. With one slow inhale, she continued into the living room. Continued closer to him.

Rissa walked over to the sofa and dropped into the armchair next to him. The one closest to his residual limb. But she wasn't looking at his leg, she was staring at his face. He figured his expression must be fierce, manifesting all the anger and rage he'd been spewing, if only in his mind and plain to see.

"Can't sleep?" she asked quietly.

John fought the urge to massage the ball of his knee. No need to draw attention to it. Even in the dark of night, her hair mussed from bed—and holy hell there was a place his brain did not need to go—she exuded an inner grace and ethereal beauty. When she wasn't speaking she had a fragility that was counter to her take-charge attitude.

The primal urge to mess up that serenity, to savage that beauty, boiled inside him. So he forced himself to break his gaze from hers and rein in those desires that only seemed to grow the longer he spent in her company. What had she asked? Couldn't sleep?

"Yeah." He wanted to talk about his feelings as much as he wanted to show her his stump. But they were, in fact, partners and if she needed to talk he needed to listen. "You okay?"

He wondered if she were reliving her freak-out at the strip club.

"Um, yeah." Rissa shifted her gaze to the blank television. She rubbed her biceps. He took the opportunity to stare hungrily at her. Her supple flesh was hidden beneath a large white men's T-shirt and masculine flannel shorts in a black and light gray plaid. Not sexy. Except the outfit revealed her smooth, sleek thighs, and the outline of her pert nipples beneath the worn cotton shirt was visible even in the very dim lighting. He wasn't sure but he thought she flushed.

Suddenly the room seemed warm, close. Her scent, the subtle aroma of pure sexy woman, wafted in the air, as if her skin had heated and released the perfume to tantalize. To tempt.

His cock rose unbidden as she shivered in the warm air.

The scent hit his nose, and his body responded as if

she'd stood up and done a strip tease. What the hell was wrong with him? *Partner, partner*, he silently chanted, even as his body shouted *sexy, sexy, sex*. The drumbeat in his blood got louder and louder with each pulse of his cock.

Shit. Abstinence suddenly seemed like a terrible idea. And double, triple shit, his boner was going to be evident soon. If she moved her head even a bit, she'd see the fucking wood he was sporting.

And there was nothing he could conveniently use to cover the club in his shorts.

Which sucked. Because A: she wouldn't possibly want to get with him, and B: he hadn't had sex since before his injury.

It was going to be awkward as hell whenever he finally got around to it.

And marring her perfection with his ugly body was not going to happen. No matter how much his cock stood up and begged.

She leaned forward until her elbows were on her knees. Which would have been fine except now she seemed hyper-focused on the coffee table. But if she lifted her gaze at all she was going to get an eyeful of his erection.

Because the monster just seemed to keep growing.

"Want to talk about it?" The last fucking he thing he wanted to do but hopefully if he kept her talking she wouldn't notice his very obvious attraction.

Her low laugh trilled. "God, no."

Which should have made him feel better. But when she laughed, a puff of breath blew against his thigh. And he couldn't help but think about how close she was.

Heat rose between them.

She had her fists clenched tightly.

It had been a really, really long time since he'd had sex.

Longer than he cared to think about. And suddenly all he could think about was the fact that she was close enough to reach out and touch.

"How about you?" she asked. There was a note in her voice he couldn't place. But the husky rasp skittered over his nerve endings.

"How about me what?"

"Anything you want to…talk about?" She dropped her gaze to his lap. Instead of freezing him with an ice-queen glare, her intense stare was hot. She licked her lips and he was pretty damn sure that it was an unconscious gesture. She was as stiff as his cock and he could feel the intensity radiating from her.

He had an idea where she was going and he couldn't for the life of him figure out why.

"What are you doing?" His tone was harsh, almost accusatory. Because damn, he wanted her. And if she didn't hightail it back to her side of the suite PDQ, he was going to do something they'd both regret.

"Nothing, apparently." She laughed again but this time it was embarrassed.

She stumbled to her feet. But she'd gotten up so fast that she overbalanced and began to fall forward. If he didn't catch her, she was going to land right on his stump.

John jerked and reached out to catch her as she pitched toward the coffee table.

He caught her at the elbow, her skin silky beneath his rougher palms.

But his hold had thrown her more off balance and now she was headed for the sofa and his lap.

In a second, she'd planted her hands on the opposite side of his hips, her ass was sticking up in the air, right at his eye level, and her T-shirt had gaped open enough for him to see her bare, generous breasts. It was too dark to make out the color but her nipples were hard little buttons.

"Sheesh." She exhaled in another puff of breath.

John froze. He didn't move a single muscle. He barely even breathed. The only sound he could hear was the rush of blood through his veins.

John's gaze was riveted on her breasts. His mouth watered, and his body reacted predictably to the sight of all those lush female curves mere inches from his lips, hardening even further with a powerful rush of blood to all the pertinent and long unused places.

Rissa didn't move either.

Then, she dropped her head down, her hair tumbling around her face and hiding her from him. Her shoulders hunched and her gaze was now firmly fixed on the tent in his shorts. The ends of her hair brushed the bare skin of his thigh.

He huffed out an embarrassed breath.

Fuck.

He could feel every pound of his heartbeat in his cock. And he wanted out but he was trapped effectively by the cage of her body. There was no way to get up and away until she moved.

Heat rose from his body as he reacted to the nearness of hers.

Until finally the temptation was too much. John lifted his rough hand, staring almost as if it was attached to someone else, as if he were watching some other guy think about touching her. With a gentle curl of his fingers, he brushed her black hair away from the curve of her cheek so that he could see her face.

Goddamn. He wanted. So fucking much.

She'd inhaled. Didn't seem to be breathing. Was barely moving, poised over him.

Had she shifted closer?

Anticipation shimmered in the silent room.

John leaned forward. Her eyes drifted closed. He paused when they were barely an inch apart. Her sweet minty breath whispered over his mouth. John finally closed the distance between them and pressed his lips to hers. He sucked the plump curve of her bottom lip lightly into his mouth. The contact was gentle but not tentative. His touch far surer than he felt. No hesitation. No uncertainty.

He kissed her, his thumb brushing over her cheek and his other palm cupping her jaw with an exquisite tenderness. Treating her as if she were fragile, taking care not to hurt her.

He couldn't think past how good this felt.

He gave her time to pull away. But damn he hoped and prayed she wouldn't. Heat, desire wrapped around them in the intimate darkness like a cloak protecting them from outside threat.

Rissa lifted her palm to his bare shoulder and he shuddered. Then she broke the kiss and pushed slightly away from him. Her face was shadowed as she perched, one hand on the couch next to his hip and her other soft against the ball of his shoulder. She stared into his eyes, her gaze questioning, hesitant.

The only sound in the room was their harsh breathing. Far too harsh for the light kiss they'd shared.

Rissa's chest heaved in and out, her fingers clenched against his bare skin. But what slayed him was the expression in her eyes. They were mostly in the dark. The glow of the light from the stove cast an uneven reflection over their silhouettes. But John could see the naked vulnerability in her gaze.

His own likely wasn't much better.

John was used to action. Used to kicking ass and taking names but he'd lost some of that mojo when he'd lost his leg.

He sat there, giving her the control to choose what happened next, hoping she'd choose to stay, before doubts and insecurity could kick in and she'd retreat.

Right now he wasn't thinking about logistics or how awkward it was going to be. Right now he was waiting for the green light and then maybe he'd worry about that stuff. Because right now all he could think about was sinking into her wet heat.

Of reveling in the welcoming clasp of her body. Of drowning in sex. Of losing himself in physical pleasure. Because it had been so damn long.

But the next move was up to her.

RISSA TEETERED on the edge of reason.

This was a bad idea. Really bad. Her head wasn't in a good place. She wasn't even sure his head was in the right space.

Light from between the small gap in the curtains slanted across his face and highlighted his eyes. And the hope in his hazel gaze struck a chord deep within her.

His skin was supple beneath her palm. Rissa hesitated one more moment, then decided to let everything go. They both needed this.

She'd been attracted to him from the moment they'd met. She just hadn't thought they'd ever have the opportunity to get this physically close. But now that she was here, she didn't want to waste the chance.

She glanced down at his legs, for a second unsure if it would hurt if she sat on his lap. Then she mentally shrugged. He wasn't shy. He'd move her if she was causing him any pain. So Rissa swung her right leg over his lap and then knelt over him on the sofa. Her knees bracketed his hips and she braced both hands instinctively on his shoulders. His broad, muscular, naked shoulders.

John let out a long, slow sigh and tilted his head back against the sofa. "Thank fuck."

For some reason his obvious relief loosened the tightness of insecurity and she let out a little chuckle.

John's big hands came to her hips and he settled her on his thighs. A sense of peace descended over her as other impressions registered. The nubby texture of the sofa on her knees and calves, his silky shorts beneath her butt, and the scratchiness of the hair on his thighs as he slid her along his legs until he cradled her hips with his.

The thick length of his erection rubbed against her swollen and throbbing sex. And she suddenly understood that whole historical-romance notion of swooning because her head went light and she practically melted into him.

With one small tug, she fell against his chest. Her breasts smashed against his hard muscles.

John let out a groan as she pressed against his heat. Rissa's fists had flattened out and she was caressing his shoulders in slow, languorous strokes. Goose bumps peppered his skin.

And he stared into her eyes, the moment fraught with an unexpected tension. She'd made the first move so now she figured it was his turn. But he was perfectly still, no action. Finally, she nudged him.

"You going to kiss me or what?"

John angled his head and dove into the kiss.

She'd spread her hips wide and their bodies synced as if they'd done this a thousand times together. He kissed her like time had stopped, stalled, and everything faded away except the sensual details, wrapping them in a cocoon of intimacy.

He cupped her hips in his large palms and edged his thumbs beneath her T-shirt, rubbing lightly against her waist. His callused fingers whispered along her skin, and her body clenched, hungry for him. Hungry for something more than this delicate touch.

Her nipples tightened to nearly painful buds as he leisurely nipped at her mouth. His naked skin was supple and warm beneath her touch. Arousal pulsed deep and low in her body.

She nibbled at his mouth, urging him to move faster, kiss her harder. But as if she had pushed a button, he slowed down. He skated one palm over her hip and along her thigh. Everything clenched. Then he slid his hand back, coming perilously closer to where she needed him. She gripped him by the jaw and jammed her mouth over his.

"So impatient," he murmured against her lips.

"It's been a while," she confessed, trying to let him know she was on the edge. Sexual frustration was making her crazy. Because she was one step away from grabbing him and inhaling him.

He cleared his throat, lifted his gaze. His hazel eyes glowed in the dimly lit room, the expression on his face was wry. "Me too."

They held there, on the precipice.

Breath mingled. Anticipation was heavy in the heated air.

She slid her fingers through the short strands of his black hair and scraped her nails over his scalp, and let triumph roar when he groaned again and lifted his hips so his cock rubbed against her clit. Their admissions unleashed the restrained passion.

She slid her palms down his muscular chest and abs, and his muscles flexed beneath her hands even as he skimmed her T-shirt up and over her head.

John lifted his palms to her breasts and cupped them in his hands. His thumbs rubbed over her distended nipples and her body liquefied. He leaned forward and sucked one nipple into his mouth. The hot suction zapped electricity straight to her clit as he sucked voraciously on one nipple while his hand played intently with the other.

Electricity tingled through her from the twin assaults, his attention pushing her toward a spectacular orgasm. But she didn't want to go over that edge alone.

The tip of his cock pushed from the waist of his basketball shorts and glistened with a drop of pre-come.

Rissa rubbed her thumb over the head of his cock and slipped her hand beneath the elastic. She curled her fingers around his impressive girth and caught her breath at the thought of that thick long cock inside her.

She squeezed and he pulled his mouth from her breast.

"Goddamn, Riss," he wheezed. "You're killing me."

"But what a way to go, huh?" she teased, slightly surprised by the playfulness. She wasn't usually comfortable enough during sex to relax enough to play.

She pushed his shorts down to completely expose his penis. A nest of dark curls framed his impressive thickness as his cock jutted up between them.

"I want," she said.

"Hell, yes." John shoved at her shorts. It hit them at the

same time that she was going to have to stand up to get her shorts off. Rissa scrambled off his lap and shoved her shorts to the floor. She should have been at least slightly uncomfortable standing in front of him completely naked. But his appreciative hot, crazy stare made her feel powerful, like a goddess.

"You are so fucking beautiful."

Exterior beauty is fleeting. "It's what is on your inside that's beautiful," she murmured, thinking of his strength, his peace.

Her gaze skimmed over him, the scars and nicks that decorated his body like medals of honor. She traced them with her gaze and then her fingers, touching lightly on all those imperfections, anointing them with a gentle caress to show him how much she appreciated his sacrifice. Until her hand skimmed down his left leg. "So much honor inside you. I respect you so much."

He curled his fingers around her wrist tightly. "We need a condom," he ground out.

Wow, she'd been so caught up in John's inner light, she'd completely forgotten protection. Rissa was on the pill but even as hot as he was she didn't know him well enough to go bareback. No glove, no love.

But she also hadn't come prepared. "Do you have one?" In her head she was begging. *Please, please say yes.* But she waited for him to answer.

"Yeah." He reached for the crutches.

She parroted his earlier words back at him. "Thank fuck."

That broke the sudden tension that had permeated the room and he smiled. She placed her hand over his. "Let me get it."

His mouth tightened but he nodded, then told her where he had a stash.

She wanted to run but she sauntered to his room, swinging her hips in a little taunt, just to keep his mind on her ass, rather than the fact that he needed her to go get protection.

Once she was in the bathroom Rissa hurried, knowing that if she took too long her own brain would start churning with doubt and all the things that could go south by taking this step. She hadn't had sex in over a year. Her whole life had been in a holding pattern, and this felt like moving forward. Like breaking the chains that held her back and freeing herself.

Clutching the little foil packet, she walked back into the living room. Her breath stopped in her throat when she saw him again.

For a moment she was struck by his beauty. Her heart thundered and her pulse roared in her head. He was male perfection. All that strength and confidence wrapped in muscles and displayed in the proud jut of his cock. He'd lost his shorts, the dusting of hair on his thighs and a happy trail across his pecs framed an impressive erection.

She swallowed. "Mercy," she whispered. Her gaze continued to scroll over his physique, noting the flex of his powerful thighs. Angry scars marred both legs and finally she let herself look at the open space left by his missing limb. She couldn't take her gaze away from his body as she ripped open the condom packet.

Rissa didn't give him time to be self-conscious because she feared it would happen. She deftly rolled the super-size condom over his erection and leaned in to kiss him.

His hands cupped her ass and guided her to his cock.

He held her, supporting most of her weight, and good

God, he was strong. Her hands scraped against his scalp and she commanded, "Do it." *Please*.

She wasn't above begging.

She was slick with her arousal, and even though he was big, she wouldn't have any problems taking him inside her.

Still he took care with her. John lowered her slowly onto his erection. The head parted her folds and separated her flesh as he filled her to bursting. When she was seated fully on top of him, impaled by the thick staff, John's hands skimmed over her flesh and clasped her hips. Rissa's clit pulsed against the firm muscles of his abdomen as he began to rock. John pushed up inside her, hitting her g-spot, rubbing the buried button that ramped her up to another dimension.

She gripped his biceps, holding on tight as he took her for the ride of her life. The motion started off slowly but as they rocked together, each downward slide she hit a little harder, and he pushed up a little faster until they were slamming together. She bounced on top of him, her breasts bobbing and jiggling until he cupped them and pinched her nipples every time she hit his pubic bone, coming down hard.

God she was so damn close to imploding.

He grew impossibly bigger, thicker, harder inside her.

She clenched, every nerve ending sizzling with the sensation. She gasped for oxygen, trying to draw in a breath, but the air was stifling, pheromones and lust shot from their pores and surrounded them in a haze.

Suddenly John pushed up even harder, pummeling her, until he threw back his head as his orgasm took him, catapulting him over the edge into the abyss. The muscles in his arms strained as he held her to him and the pulses deep inside her body sent her into the stratosphere. She contracted around his cock, milking him hard, her body buzzing. Her orgasm was nearly painful in release. She groaned and bent to kiss him, holding on for dear life as sensations battered her from her head to her toes, and her sex contracted with vicious pulls on his still-hard cock. Her nipples hurt, so sharp with arousal, that she rubbed against him to relieve this aching buzz that shimmered and sizzled through her. She was deaf, dumb, blind as colors and light burst behind her eyes and rendered her insensate to everything but him.

Rissa slumped against his hard chest, panting in sharp, tight breaths as she tried to come down from the insane endorphin rush that flooded her body with well-being and happiness.

He curved his arms around her back, caressing her skin with sure long strokes, as if he could soothe her through the violence of her release.

He cradled her, the embrace sweet, tender, and so unlike the explosion of passion that had erupted between them. His heart thumped beneath her cheek, skin damp with sweat, and still flushed with arousal.

"God, you feel good." His breath puffed in her ear, and a shiver rolled over her like the waves in the pool of Treasure Island.

Her body was lax with satisfaction and spent desire. She lay against his chest, letting his near sweet caress lull her into a state of lethargy.

He didn't seem inclined to move yet either.

So they sat, him still buried deep inside her, and her surrounding him, her knees outside his hips and her arms draped over his shoulders.

"You too." She nuzzled his neck and resisted the urge to nip on his earlobe. To mark him in some way.

The intimacy of what they'd done still hadn't hit her. Him either, if she was gauging him correctly. Because she was pretty sure he'd bolt as soon as the reality of their nakedness hit him. It didn't take a trained observer, which she was, to figure out that he wasn't comfortable baring his amputated leg to anyone.

While she thought he was sexy as hell, she didn't know if he'd actually believe her assertions even though they had indulged in torrid sex. And the last thing she wanted to do was embarrass him.

Rissa could feel him start to tense up. Reality was going to intrude soon. But she figured she could offer something that just might ease his disquiet. "Right after I got out of the hospital, I…tried to drown out the chaos in my head with sex."

He didn't say a word but his arms tightened around her.

"It didn't work." Rissa laughed, the sound full of disgust rather than amusement. "If anything it made it worse."

He cleared his throat. "Why?" His voice rough from disuse or embarrassment? She didn't know.

She shrugged. "Every time I had an orgasm I felt guilty. Because I was alive to have an orgasm and my partner wasn't."

"That's, um…."

"Fucked up. I know." Rissa sighed. "That's why I stopped having sex."

"So what made you change your mind?"

She hesitated again. He wasn't being a dick but he also hadn't relaxed at all. She definitely hadn't chosen her sexual partners with any discrimination right after the incident. And suddenly the idea of baring her soul was far more intimate than baring her body.

"I want to make a joke about being horny," she murmured against his skin.

"Would it really be a joke?"

"Nope. Definitely horny." But that wasn't why she'd had sex with him.

"And?"

"My partner would have liked you," she said. "You're a protector. A warrior. Worthy."

The silence was absolute.

"Too early for the truth, huh?" She tried to play it off. "In the spirit of full confession, random hookups had been my drug of choice. Until I finally figured out that wasn't helping me heal. And I owed it, *owed* it, to him to live a worthwhile life."

"A worthwhile life," he murmured with wonder.

She doubted he even knew he'd said the words aloud. He seemed lost in his thoughts. And based on anatomy, it was time for her to get off him.

She was reluctant to disengage their bodies.

She wanted to crawl into his bed with him and let him hold her and she could hold him. But he wouldn't let her get that close. And she had a responsibility to Maria. A job to return to even if this had been an absolutely magnificent interlude from her responsibilities.

He kissed the tip of each breast, then tilted her head down and kissed her forehead. Her forehead. Not exactly an erogenous zone.

And she wondered if he was sending her back to her camp.

"Thank you." He brushed his lips over hers. Then he pushed her to her feet and handed her the pajamas. "Go on back to your room. I'll handle the cleanup."

As if what they'd done was some sort of toxic waste

accident instead of spectacular sex. For a second she thought he was going to swat her on the ass and give her a shove toward the room.

But at the last minute he gave her a "well, this is awkward" smile and chin lift.

And she finally got the hint.

CHAPTER 8

Seven o'clock in the morning and the temps were already in the low 90s. John ran on the high school track, his running blade prosthetic springing against the recycled rubber. Sweat poured down his face as he pushed his body to the limit. When he'd first gotten out of Walter Reed, even with his daily physical therapy sessions, he'd been ridiculously weak. And he couldn't stand it.

His body had always been a tool he could count on. Yes, he had days where his muscles were on fire and his phantom limb ached but he wasn't about to let that fucking IED stop him. A fierce satisfaction roared through him when he hit mile ten. His muscles strained and his shorts were soaked with sweat as he pushed on. "Ooh rah."

He'd slept like shit.

He'd alternated between reliving the mind-blowing sex and Rissa's final words, "a worthwhile life."

Though it had been a while, John still acknowledged that last night had been the best sex of his life. She'd blown the top off his head, and gotten him over the hump of that first sexual encounter. He'd been a little unsteady without his prosthetic on but he'd managed her on his lap with relative ease and little discomfort. Based on how hard she'd come, he'd wager she hadn't even thought about the lack of his leg.

Her whispered confession had been the other tip of that seesaw teetering back and forth in his brain.

He needed to find the honor in his life again. First he'd have to start with not having sex with Rissa again. Sadly, he didn't think banging his coworker was honorable. He was sure Jack would see it that way too. And John didn't want to emulate his own father, a man who seemingly couldn't keep his dick in his pants, seeing as he had five adult children with four different women. John wanted to be like the fictional, made-up father his mother had told him about, not his true train wreck of a father.

John started his cool-down laps, knowing he needed to get back to the suite. He was determined to take Rissa and Maria to the shooting range.

Who would show up this morning? BB or the sweeter, more vulnerable Rissa? John slowed his pace, thinking about her mercurial moods, and realizing as he finished slowing his heart rate and loosening his muscles, that he didn't really care which Rissa showed up. He liked them both.

Which sucked since he'd just figured out that more sex with Rissa was off the table.

As much as he liked Rissa, she and Bliss were friends which meant awkwardness when they stopped having sex. If John had read Jack correctly, he was considering partnering with Rissa's employer on more jobs which also meant he couldn't do anything to jeopardize that relationship either.

After driving back to their hotel, he climbed the stairs to the third floor and headed to the suite. His shirt was hooked in the waist of his shorts and he reveled in the cool air blowing from the ceiling vents.

Before he could hold the card over the sensor, the door to the suite burst open and Rissa barreled into him.

"Oof." She bounced off his chest even as he grabbed her elbows to stop her from falling on her ass.

"I am not normally this clumsy…." She stalled, her gaze riveted to his chest.

John couldn't help but be amused, and flattered, by her distraction.

The air around them thickened, a languid intensity hovered in the atmosphere, and John's muscles expanded under her heated gaze. Rissa lazily raised her gaze to meet his, her aquamarine eyes cloudy with arousal.

John indolently skimmed his fingers from her elbow up to her shoulder and back down again. His lids drooped as a slight smile quirked his lips. Here was another Rissa. A little soft, a lot flustered, and clearly at a loss for words.

"Steady now?"

Rissa blinked, took a step back, breaking his light hold. Her invisible armor settled over her like a shell and that sweet, soft woman disappeared.

"Yeah." She was totally lying. Her husky voice betrayed how he affected her. "Thanks."

He studied Rissa. She was back in her mannish business attire again. A barrier against the world. Against him? "Give me twenty to shower and we can head out."

She quivered, her eyelids flinched. Subtly. But he'd seen it. "Not necessary."

John took a step toward Rissa until they were nearly toe to blade. "Yeah. It is."

He hated to push. Knew how much it sucked to be backed into a corner over something you didn't want to do.

But he also knew that she needed to figure out what her limitations were. He also knew that if he put it that way, she'd cut off his balls and serve them for breakfast.

"We're taking Maria too," John continued, not giving her time to argue. "You were right. She needs to start getting out."

"You can't make that decision for her." *For me* was what she was really saying.

"And I'm not." John took his shirt from the waist of his shorts and rubbed the cotton over his hair. "Connor called me while I was on my way home from the track. Maria wants to start taking back more control of her life. I guess getting freaked out yesterday pissed her off rather than sent her cowering."

John was in awe of her fortitude. Maria could give ballsy lessons to anyone.

With that he knew Rissa wouldn't protest any more. After knowing her for only one day, he knew there was no way in hell she'd let her own perceived inadequacies negatively impact Maria.

"Fine." Rissa crossed her arms over her chest, hiding her body from his hungry gaze.

Somehow they'd bulldozed right past the awkward morning-after convo.

"How are you feeling today?" he asked silkily, unable to let her go without some sort of acknowledgement of their intimacy. Which was stupid. Hadn't he just decided that last night had to be a one-time deal? He couldn't afford to jeopardize his relationship with his brother, or the business relationship his brother was building with Adams-Larsen.

She rolled her eyes at him, clearly not about to give him the satisfaction of stroking his ego. "I'll let Maria know we're leaving soon." She headed toward her room without another glance. Her absolute avoidance of him flashed like a neon sign as bright as the night sky of Vegas, telling him she remembered last night too.

Then John sighed.

Based on the way she was avoiding him, she was on the same page. Last night was a sensual detour that neither could afford to take again. No matter how much their bodies wanted them to.

He had hoped that their explosive encounter would have eased the need that dogged him relentlessly whenever he was around Rissa, but if anything his desire had increased.

The impulse to press her up against the granite breakfast bar and immerse in her scent and the sweet feminine clasp of her body surged through him.

Can't go there again. Damn but that sucked. While he'd been missing sex, it had been a sort of a "back of his mind, need to get back on the horse" nagging at him rather than a constant ache. But after last night, his body was fully on board with repeating the process.

"I'll be out of the shower and ready to go. Meet you back here."

She paused at the connecting door to her side of the suite. Her body was stiff with tension. "Okay."

John headed for his shower. His cold shower.

Rissa hustled into the room she shared with Maria. She closed the interconnecting door gently, then leaned back against the hard surface and willed her thundering heartbeat to slow. Holy Mother of God. When all that hard male flesh had been inches away, she'd had to physically stop herself from leaning into him and licking his damp skin.

He was perfection. Michelangelo would have begged to

sculpt him, Michael Stokes would beg to photograph him. Her hands trembled as she swept her hair into a ponytail, holding the thick fall off her neck to cool down.

"Everything okay?"

Rissa yelped.

"I didn't mean to scare you," Maria said gently.

"No. Not you, me." Rissa refused to let Maria take the fall for her wandering thoughts. "I was just…." She blushed. *She. Blushed.*

When was the last time she'd gotten that flustered by a guy?

Maria blinked. The skin around her dark eyes crinkled in amusement as she glanced at the door behind Rissa's back. "Ay-yi-yi, as my mama used to say."

"Excuse me?"

"John without his shirt on." Maria waved her hand in front of her face, fanning herself, and her amused gaze shifted to the door again. "He's hot."

"I assure you Maria, there is nothing untoward going on," Rissa said stiffly. Could the stick get further up her ass?

Maria flicked her hand. "I don't care if you two hook up."

Rissa started to protest that they weren't hooking up but that wasn't actually true. They'd been…involved last night, that was for sure. So she kept silent. "I won't let anything affect your safety," she finally ground out.

Rissa wasn't even sure what last night was all about. Relieving tension, sure. But in the protective darkness their passion had felt like something more. Like they'd connected on a level she'd never felt before.

Which was bullshit.

That must be some weird hormone endorphin buzz from the magnificent orgasm he'd bestowed upon her.

Maria just smirked.

Rissa blew out a breath. "You want to go to the gun range?" She posed it as a question, hoping, praying that Maria would deny it and give Rissa an out.

Yeah, that made her a coward but she wasn't ready. Her heart was pounding and her head was light. And it wasn't from anything so exciting as sex. It was straight-up fear.

But the Universe didn't hear her plea, because Maria nodded. "Yes. I want to learn how to shoot a gun."

And there went her excuse. Rissa would never inhibit Maria. She'd been a hostage to too many other people in her life, however Rissa wanted to make sure that Maria had a handle on her reasons.

"Learning to shoot won't necessarily make you safer," Rissa cautioned. "It's a good skill to have in your toolbox but you still have to stay vigilant."

"I know." She had the impression that Maria was mentally rolling her eyes at her.

"Okay, good. John will be ready soon."

Thud, thud, thud. The door trembled behind her back. "I guess he's ready now."

Maria smiled, her entire face lit up with an ethereal glow. For a moment Rissa envied her, that simple joy shone through, the fear and the terror she'd endured nowhere to be seen. "I'm ready."

Maria speared her with one last ironic glance that seemed to ask, *Are you?*

Of course the answer was unequivocally…hell, no.

JOHN BRACED for the deafening bang of gunfire. He knew coming to the range would be difficult for Rissa but he wanted to help her. He hadn't really counted on how hard it would be for him either. He hadn't been in combat, hadn't been anywhere near people discharging firearms, since he'd been blown up.

"We aren't going to need weapons on this op." Rissa was still trying to stop this from happening.

"Maybe." This was a major US city, not the Helmand Province. The odds of a shootout with bad guys, assuming they were even on the right track to find the bad guys, was about a million to one. "But before I was a Marine I was a Boy Scout. And I take that shit seriously," he said with a completely straight face.

Rissa snickered and her shoulders relaxed. Mission accomplished.

"Start with a .22." John placed the little pea shooter in her hand carefully, his fingers wrapped around hers, the weapon pointed toward the dirt floor. Her skin was warm beneath his and he flashed back to last night when her hand was wrapped around something far more intimate.

The sensual heat in her blue-green eyes told him she was remembering the same thing.

Thinking about last night was far more pleasurable than thinking about firing the weapon. He also knew she needed to do this.

The cement lane buffered the sound of gunfire from the other patrons but he still had to brace himself for the sharp bursts hitting his ears like thumps to the chest. And he remembered last night in that strip club. How Rissa had completely freaked at the noise. The impulse to comfort her made his palms itch.

John grabbed the ear protectors hanging around his neck, held on to the ear muffs to stop from reaching for her.

He leaned in, their torsos nearly touching. His lips

brushed the shell of her ear, the contact a straight zap to his cock.

"Last night." He glanced away from her, at the target hanging fifty yards out. Damn, he'd rather be back at Camp Leatherneck than have this conversation. "I froze for a second."

The confession was ripped from his depths.

Her surprised gaze caught his.

He nodded. It was true. He'd completely lost where he was for a second, but then he saw Rissa freaking out and he tore himself out of his own memories to help her. "But you needed me and I pulled it together."

Rissa's eyes were wide with shock.

"If someone else was in danger, you'd handle it." He had no doubts.

John took a deliberate step back, then set the box of ammunition on the table next to her. "I'm going next door to work with Maria." He figured she'd want to be alone anyway.

John headed out before her hesitant vulnerability caused him to do something inadvisable.

Rissa nodded and turned away from him without another word. He only hoped his admission had helped.

RISSA DIDN'T WANT to watch John walk away.

His confession had surprised her and she knew a moment of shame for still being afraid. She stared at the matte-black finish of the small firearm. A .22 was the most innocuous of weapons. The rounds could do some damage up close but as a defensive weapon, most LEOs picked something with a little more firepower.

And yet, her heart was beating so hard in her chest, her

fear drowned out everything but the overwhelming sounds of the range. Every bang, every round fired, rolled over her like a tsunami crashed over land and wiped out everything until she was isolated by her fear.

Cordite stung her nose. The taste lingered on her tongue. The scent of the desert, mesquite and sand, underlaid the smells of weapons being discharged and her own sweat. The gunpowder residue burned her eyes, yeah, that's why she was tearing up. The lie clogged her throat.

"This is stupid, Riss," she berated herself. "Lift up the damn gun and aim."

She tried to raise her arm. But she was shaking so hard that she was afraid she'd accidentally pull the trigger and the shot would go wild. Obviously the cement lanes prohibited her from hurting anyone around her but still, the possibility lingered in the haunted crevasses of her brain.

She dropped her head, letting the weight pull on her neck, and closed her eyes, willing her heartbeat to slow. Carefully she braced her left hand under the grip on her right, weapon still pointed straight down at the dirt floor. Now both arms were shaking uncontrollably.

Sweat gathered at her hairline. The tension in her shoulders ramped up her stress level even as she tried to relax. Rissa inhaled slowly on a long, desperate attempt to calm, to breathe.

Dammit. She just wanted to stop being afraid. Stop hiding behind a bitchy persona. Stop painting makeup on her face to hide the ugly that festered beneath her icy demeanor.

Rissa lifted the her arms, her posture and stance textbook as she stared down the sight on the small weapon. Her arms shook. She wanted to throw up. Tears gathered in her eyes as she tried to control her breath, control her movements enough to actually release the trigger. Her index finger skimmed along the curved metal and she shook her hair away from her face. Sweat pooled under her arms and across her back.

Every new exhale, she had the chance to shoot.

But no matter how hard she tried, she couldn't make herself fire.

Memories flashed across her vision.

The warehouse, her partner, the sound of the bullets hitting his chest. The scream trapped inside as she tried desperately to save him. The gurgling gasp as blood filled his lungs and spilled across the floor. The wail of the sirens as the ambulance arrived. Sticky blood between her fingers, running in rivulets over the back of her hands as she tried frantically to hold it in his body.

The rise of bile as reality hit her. He was gone.

Rissa let her arms drop, and very, very carefully placed the weapon on the table meant to hold supplies. Then she dropped her head to the rough plywood surface and breathed slowly, trying to get back to a place where she could function. But reality was slow to return. The sounds of gunfire echoed all around her. Each report like a blow.

Two years and she still couldn't shoot a weapon. She'd known this was a bad idea.

"Hey." John's arms wrapped around her waist from behind.

She stiffened. They didn't know each other well enough for him to touch her so casually. But while she was trying to pull her invisible armor over her and get her bitchy façade in place, he was turning her around and tilting her chin up. His fingers were rough yet oh so gentle on her face.

He tenderly wiped the moisture from her cheeks while she cursed that he'd seen her cry. Dammit. Show no weakness. The last thing she needed was John Pulaski reporting back to Jack Stone that she couldn't do her job.

His gaze shifted to the blank target. Not a single hole marred the paper. "There's always next time."

A snort escaped. Next time. *Right.*

She was a weak fool. But she couldn't admit that she didn't think there would be a next time. "How did Maria do?"

She stepped back, needing the physical distance. Needing to not give in to the weakness that slithered through her. So tempted to lean into his embrace, to take comfort rather than handle her inadequacies on her own.

"Not bad." John seemed reluctant to let her go. "But she's ready to head back, if that's okay."

Rissa couldn't wait to get the hell out of here. Every single report of a weapon was the bang of a nail in the coffin of her failure. She nodded and tried to focus on the job. "We need to review any new information that Connor's been able to pull up for us anyway."

But John wouldn't let it go. "Things change," he said gently. "Maybe your new reality doesn't include firing a weapon."

His voice was understanding. She couldn't bear to see the pity that she was sure he felt.

Even though her soul was ripping apart and her heart was heavy, she tilted her chin up and gave him her patented "back off" glare. "I'll get Maria."

The writing was on the wall. She was done in the field. Done with this line of work altogether.

She would stick out this assignment. She refused to give up on Maria. She wouldn't let Jillian or Bliss down either. She'd give one hundred and ten percent to this op, and then she'd have to find a new line of work.

CHAPTER 9

When they arrived back at the suite, Jack was already there. As soon as they walked in, Jack gave Maria a hug and kissed her on the forehead. "How you doing?"

She smiled tentatively at Jack. "Good. Great actually."

John nodded. "She did really well for her first time out."

Jack squeezed her shoulder with his big palm. "Excellent."

Maria glanced around the suite. "Where's Bliss?"

"Ah, I came over on my own." Read: he'd left Bliss behind.

Maria looked quizzical. "Oh."

"Listen, Ava wanted you to call her." Jack handed Maria a slip of paper. "Here's her room at the Palazzo."

"Okay." Maria shifted her gaze between them, clearly sensing the tension in the room. She lifted the paper. "I'll just go call her in the other room."

Once Maria went through the connecting door, Jack said, "We need to talk."

John raised his eyebrows, clearly taken aback by Jack's

harsh tone. Rissa was surprised he was here again and wondered if they'd had a break in the investigation.

"Bliss told me about last night."

Last night?

Panic fluttered in her belly. How could Bliss know about her and John having sex? She hadn't told a soul. It certainly wasn't her most professional moment. Shit. Way to represent Adams-Larsen. Jillian was going to kick her ass.

All that flittered through her mind, rapid-fire, until she comprehended there was no way he was talking about her and John.

Further back, Riss.

Crap, he was talking about the club. Jeez, she was three catastrophes out from the initial freak from fireworks. But she sure wasn't going to share that tidbit with Jack.

Her private shame was on public display and up for discussion. She felt out of control. whirling, reeling from one hit after another. She waited for John to admit that she'd broken down at the gun range too.

"She handled it." John frowned at Jack. "*We* handled it."

Rissa could have fallen to her knees and kissed him. Then other things she could do on her knees hit her frontal cortex and a full body flush spread from her toes to her hairline. Fortunately, Jack didn't notice. But John was giving her a strange look.

"I think we should take Rissa out of the field." Jack's white button-down sleeves were rolled up his forearms, his hands on his khaki-covered hips, a thick rubber dive watch emphasizing his thick muscular wrist.

John immediately replied, "No. Not happening."

Jack paced the suddenly crowded-feeling living area. "You can continue alone. Say your wife is having second thoughts or she's sick. We can come up with something believable."

John didn't even hesitate. "Not a chance. We need her."

Rissa was silent, watching it play out. She wanted to protest, say she'd be fine. But what if she wasn't? What if she jeopardized John's safety?

The tension in the room had escalated from zero to Mach three in seconds.

Jack and John faced off. Both men had bulked up, hands on their hips, and their expressions were hard, uncompromising masks. The family resemblance was there in the jut of their jaw and the shape of their eyes. Jack was the epitome of well-dressed businessman, while John's more casual cargo pants and polo shirt emphasized the breadth of his shoulders and the thickness of his biceps. Both alpha, but each with their own distinct edge.

"She can handle it," John defended her. "We have a solid lead. We can't let it disappear."

John was right. They couldn't afford to waste this opportunity.

Hadn't she just recommitted to seeing this operation through? "I'll be okay." Rissa thought she understood Jack's worry. "I've got John's back."

Jack flicked his hand. "Of course you do. But we're in a time crunch here. Once Fernandez's testimony is public, we won't have much time before this asshole, Ortega, goes to ground. He's got ties in both the US and Mexico. And he's rich enough to use an emissary to do business in the US if he's implicated. He can eliminate himself from the public eye and we'll never get the fucker."

"Does your concern mean Con has more intel for us?"

"Yeah." Jack sat down on the sofa. "Once we knew the

website, Con was able to start running searches on Ortega's possible and known aliases."

"Is the guy really that stupid?"

Jack scrunched up his face. "Um, maybe I should clarify. The government has a file on the guy but they've never been able to pin a thing on him. To most people he is just what he appears to be, a prominent legitimate Mexican businessman."

"So how did we get this intel?" Rissa asked, thankful that he seemed to have dropped wanting her out.

"It's possible that Con—" Jack placed his palms over Rissa's ears, "—went in a backdoor somewhere."

"He has a backdoor into the FBI's database?" Rissa blurted out.

Jack's grin lit his face up like a mischievous little boy's. "I never said that."

"And I didn't hear that." Rissa still had friends at the Bureau. But sometimes the end justified the means. In this case, for eight years the FBI had gotten nowhere in finding these girls. The trail had been that well-hidden. If Stone Consulting and Adams-Larsen had the chance to right this wrong, with a little help from illegally obtained information, she wasn't going to protest. She knew they wouldn't use the access for any nefarious purpose. That still didn't mean that she wanted to know the details of the method in which they procured the information.

But she did need to deliver some caution. "You need to make sure any evidence is admissible."

"We can make sure that we obtain the information legally, after the fact if need be." John tilted his head.

Rissa raised a brow. Really?

"No one has more paperwork rules and regs than the

US Military," John said. "And once you know the rules, it's easier to subvert them…without getting caught."

"Not just paperwork," Rissa said. "Everything has to be above board in order to serve warrants."

"Don't worry about that," Jack broke in. "I've got a friend who works Vice at LVPD. He'll be able to get an initial warrant based on an anonymous tip if it supports the info they already have. He says they've been searching for the right piece of evidence to cement the warrant and put it in front of a judge."

"Okay." Rissa rubbed her hands together like an evil mastermind. "So what have we got?"

Jack handed them printouts of women's profiles on Backdoor.

"Con has managed to link all these girls to a single account. After a lot of digging, he found the connection between that account and an alias believed to be Manuel Ortega. He believes the girls are part of Ortega's stable. But that's as far as he's gotten," Jack said.

Acid bubbled in Rissa's stomach, spreading sickness through her as she stared at the pictures. There were easily fifty young women's profiles in the stack. Reduced to files on a website, who knew how many of these girls were victims? Individuals who had hopes and dreams until they'd been stolen from them. She traced her finger along the edge of the paper.

"I need you guys to figure out if there's any other connection, or how we can dig deeper." Jack glanced at the watch on his wrist.

"Any facial recognition matches between the profiles and our missing women?" Rissa asked.

"Not on Sophia and Graciela. Con is working on it,"

Jack said again. "But we did get matches to some older missing teen cases on the West Coast."

"Good." John said fiercely, "But we also need to find Maria's friends."

Rissa's heart clenched. What about all the rest? The construct of safety was fragile. Just like Maria wanting to learn to shoot a gun, had all these girls once thought that something would keep them safe? One small, seemingly insignificant decision could change the course of your life.

She tuned back into the conversation just as Jack asked John, "How are *you* doing?"

John lifted his eyebrows. "What do you mean?"

"This is a little outside what you're used to." Jack flattened his palms on the breakfast bar counter. "Enough action for you?"

Rissa held her breath, oddly interested in John's reply.

JOHN TILTED his head and considered Jack's question. He didn't want to answer too quickly. So he really thought about what Jack was asking. What did he think so far?

"This job has a concrete objective. And if we can find those girls we've made a difference." That was a big *if*. But one that gave him impetus.

"The scope is smaller than your work in the military, but I can tell you that personally being able to see the impact your actions have is a hell of a rush." Jack's entire body radiated seriousness and commitment.

John could envision that. Rissa made a sound from next to him. The hardest thing when he quit being a Marine was his loss of purpose.

And just like Rissa had whispered last night, he wanted a meaningful life.

Had she moved closer?

John chose his next words carefully. Obviously he wasn't a shoe-in but he hoped that if he proved himself on this op that Jack would make his employment permanent.

"I like the possibility of making a difference almost immediately."

"Good." Jack slapped him on the back. "After I get back from my honeymoon we'll iron out all the minutiae. But consider yourself our newest employee."

John was stunned.

"But—"

"I know we discussed this as a trial but—" Jack pierced Rissa with a look "—it's come to my attention that I have way too much on my plate. And since we're making this collaboration with Adams-Larsen official, our work load is only going to increase. I need people I can trust."

Beside him Rissa stiffened.

John didn't think Jack's words were a dig at her but he didn't really know Jack that well. After all, he wouldn't have expected Jack to blindly hire him either.

"You sure you don't want to wait until we've had some success?" John didn't want Jack to regret his decision.

"I tend to make up my mind quickly," Jack said. "Comes from being in charge of the family when the old man took off. I make a decision and stick to it."

Jack had been only fourteen when the manwhore bugged out and left the four kids with Shelley. John couldn't imagine the pressure Jack had felt to be the man of the house. He'd been a damn kid.

"Right now I've got to go. I've got Con on this still but whatever help or insight you can provide would be great." Jack frowned, gave John a very intent, penetrating look. "He's...dealing with some personal stuff."

"Okay. We'll get to work on this right away."

Jack clapped John on the back and nodded curtly at Rissa. And then his cell rang.

"Bliss, babe." Jack stopped, held still. His voice softened as he said, "Slow down."

Rissa could hear her raised voice through the phone.

"Poisoned?!" Jack's movements were agitated as he raked his right hand through his hair. "Fuck. I'll be right there."

"Everything okay?" Rissa had to assume Bliss wasn't poisoned but something was clearly up.

"Shelley's problems have escalated." Jack said grimly, "We think someone tried to poison her. I've got to go."

John nodded. "We'll deal with this. You can count on us."

"Good luck," Rissa said.

Jack beelined for the door, and was gone.

Once Jack left, the room seemed to shrink and her awareness of John ripped to the forefront again. Rissa flashbacked to John and Jack next to each other at the breakfast bar. Jack had a raw power and masculine energy. But John, there was something about him that made her knees go weak.

He exuded a tough, intense vibe that made her want to prod at him and rub up against him all at once. Two such contradictory reactions, extremes, that she was constantly in an unsettled state.

"So what do you want to do?"

"You're our best resource. You've got the investigative experience." John asked, "What do you suggest?"

Rissa nearly preened. "Let's review the files first." But ideas were brewing in her head. Pretexting techniques to gather more information.

They sat side by side at the breakfast bar in the kitchen and poured over the profiles and photos of the Latina women from the Backdoor listings.

Rissa studied the photograph in her hand, trying to be objective rather than sick to her stomach, since chances were that this girl had not volunteered to be a prostitute. The shoes she wore might actually be Christian Louboutins. The expensive shoes with their signature red sole typically ran about seven hundred dollars but depending on the shoe could cost several thousand.

And if the tennis bracelet on her wrist and the studs in her ears were real, the cha-ching factor went up again.

The woman's hair was glossy, highlighted, and her skin was smooth, buffed and polished. She had a mani/pedi in cotton candy pink that perfectly matched her glossy pink lipstick.

Rissa catalogued the details in the photo, sifting through the pieces in her brain. This was no low-budget, shoddy operation. Expensively kept. Groomed. These girls were decked out in high-end designers.

"So what does this mean?" John held up a picture of a woman dressed in a bustier with garters and stockings and little innocent-looking ribbons in strategic places. She'd seen that exact outfit, without the woman licking a dildo, in a La Perla catalogue. The entire outfit retailed for a cool fifteen hundred. "In Call?"

"The client goes to their place." Rissa explained. "Out call, they come to you."

John frowned. "Seems dangerous."

Rissa raised an eyebrow.

"For them," John countered. "Wouldn't it make them vulnerable because their clients know where they live?"

"I assume they don't have a choice." It would be easier

for their handler to control them too if the girls weren't allowed to leave.

They continued to page through the offerings. The services varied from profile to profile. Threesomes, blow jobs, lap dances, erotic dances, companionship, massage therapists….

"Happy ending," John blurted. "I'm aware of what that means."

Rissa flushed. They'd both gotten their happy ending last night. Her gaze furtively slipped to the sofa behind them.

"We can guess what full service is," John said grimly. "But how are we going to link these girls to Ortega if we pay them directly?"

"You don't know that we pay them directly," Rissa shot back. The payment terms were not listed on the information page. "We need Con to trace the links on their page accounts."

This was turning out to be a more technical job than she'd anticipated. Although these days, everything led to needing tech skills.

But there was one thing they needed to do that was totally old school. Rissa's stomach soured. "You know we need to show these pictures to Maria."

John's mouth flattened. "Yeah. Fuck."

Her thoughts too. She hated it. Even though Con had facial recognition programs, they needed Maria to see if any of these women stood out.

She must be off the phone with Ava but she hadn't come out from their bedroom. That was not going to be a fun conversation.

Rissa shuffled through the pictures again and tapped the

photos. "Did you notice that all of these women offer In Call services?"

"You think there's a connection?"

"Maybe not, but why don't we try to make a few appointments and see what we get?"

Rissa considered the setup. Basically they would be pretexting these women but she didn't see any way around it, and since they weren't planning to use this particular operation to prosecute anyone, they should be okay.

"Couple, seeking a third sexual partner for a night." Wasn't this awkward? Would it have been any less awkward if they hadn't had sex? She didn't know. Probably. Maybe. But even if they hadn't, she wanted him. Which would have made it awkward as hell.

John snapped his fingers. "You like to watch, rather than participate."

He doubted her ability. "You don't think I can handle it?"

"Uh, no. Pretty much thought you're the trained investigator, if I can keep the woman busy while you 'watch,' you can snoop, then we can accumulate more data." John paused. "But we can always go with girl on girl and I want to watch."

For a moment she was tempted to argue on general principle but that was stupid and he was right. "No, you got this."

So John got on the phone. They made their requirements clear upfront and set up several appointments using multiple fake names.

After the third phone call, John very carefully pressed the end-call button on his phone. "The address was the same for every girl. Even the instructions are the same.

'Doorman will vet you and let you upstairs.' So we know where they live but not which apartment."

"So these women *are* all connected. Now we just have to figure out if they are really connected to Ortega." Rissa rubbed her palm over the glossy granite countertop.

"Let's try a few more," John suggested. "So we have a solid sampling of the profiles that Connor identified."

After another seven phone calls they had their answer. All but one of the women lived in the same apartment building. "This can't be coincidence."

John was ready to jump from his stool and storm the apartment complex. Probably leftover from his days as a Marine. But Rissa knew they needed to be more cautious.

"We still shouldn't jump to conclusions." Rissa analyzed the data they did have. All of their "dates" were for tomorrow night. "We don't want to tip Ortega off."

But they were all in the same complex. They went online to figure out if the building had any apartment openings that Jack and Con could set up in but they couldn't find any rental company or management firm listed for the building

"I wonder who owns it?" And why there was no listing. Even exclusive buildings tended to have a way to contact the management company, but there was nothing listed anywhere on the web.

They'd identified nine prostitutes working out of this building. "You'd think the neighbors would complain," John said.

"And the doorman has to know something is going on." Rissa tapped her mouth with her index finger.

"Unless the doorman is the pimp." John and Rissa brainstormed strategies. They needed to be visible and spend some money in the next day to cement their cover story. And they needed to show the profiles to Maria, but there was a particular buzz around the rest of their day. John could feel it. He and Rissa were on the right track. Maybe they'd finally gotten a break.

~

MARIA FINALLY CAME out of the bedroom around dinner time. Rissa wasn't looking forward to what they had to do next.

"We need to show you some pictures," Rissa said softly.

Maria's face was grim, her pretty mouth was a flat line, and her deep soulful eyes sheened with tears. "Are they dead?"

"What?" John asked. "No. Jesus. Sorry." He patted her awkwardly.

Wow they were handling this all wrong. Rissa wrapped her arm around Maria's shoulders. "Not crime scene pictures."

Maria let out a shuddering breath.

"But they are still going to be difficult to look at," Rissa said.

"I can handle it." Maria held out her hand.

Of course she could. This woman could give Rissa lessons in how to handle life. "We think the man who took your friends from Fernandez is running a prostitution ring in Las Vegas."

"Bastards." Maria firmed her mouth. "Let me see if I recognize anyone."

John gave her the profiles. She dropped heavily to the sofa. One hand over her mouth as if to stop angry curses from overflowing, she slowly studied each picture.

"There are some days—" she swallowed "—where I think I was the lucky one."

Rissa's breath stopped in her throat, humbled by Maria's response.

John said gently, "We'll get them back."

He shouldn't promise Maria, but her heart softened at his gruff determination to comfort Maria.

Rissa and John were silent as Maria looked through the pictures. She finally shook her head, her long black hair swaying across her back at the force of the gesture. "No."

Damn. It had been a long shot.

Of course it couldn't be that easy. Rissa fought the urge to slump with disappointment. Next to her, John nearly vibrated with the need to punch something.

Maria visibly stiffened her shoulders. "I take it we're staying here tonight?"

"Yeah."

"Let's watch some CSI. The bad guy always gets caught in the end." Maria's dark eyes took on a determined sparkle. "And Nick Stokes is hot."

Rissa had the oddest thought that Maria was comforting them.

CHAPTER 10

John and Rissa took their car to the Bellagio and parked in the casino garage. Dressed the part of a wealthy couple, they sauntered around for a half an hour, dropped a few thousand dollars at a craps table, thanks to the Stone family's nearly unlimited funds, and then headed for the portico.

They called an Uber, set up under their cover identities, and waited for the car.

Con had confirmed that someone had been investigating the Walkers' background. They had cancelled all the appointments except one and used their cover to confirm the appointment.

While the odds of someone tracking them at the hotel were low, they slipped into their cover personas, portraying an affectionate couple on a romantic getaway.

They had done recon on the building earlier in the day and scoped out the neighborhood. The elegant four-story apartment building appeared upscale and ritzy on the outside.

Nothing about it indicated that a prostitution ring was operating inside.

They pulled up to the building. The semi-circle covered driveway was adorned with giant pots overflowing with spikes and flowers surrounded by drooping greenery. The pots flanked a pair of large French double doors, and a jute Welcome mat shone under the discreet lighting.

"Thanks, man." John slid out of the UberBLACK limo, then held out his hand for Rissa. She extended her arm languidly and smoothly placed her hand in his. In a slow exit, her movements eerily similar to a strip tease, one elegant leg touched on the granite circular driveway.

Rissa slid her other leg out the door, her stockings shushed as her legs rubbed against each other, the move sensual and erotic. She stood beside him, the epitome of classiness and grace. Her eyes were hidden by large framed sunglasses. And he couldn't help but hug her, thankful for the brush of her body against his. She nuzzled his jaw with her nose and whispered, "Cameras at twelve, three, six and nine. We're on."

The Uber car drove away.

But John didn't move yet.

The plan had a few variables that would be difficult to predict, and he wanted to reassure her and himself. John's hand glided over the bare skin exposed by the lack of material on the back of the sexy dress, until he cupped her neck in his palm and tilted her head back.

She smiled seductively as if there were no one else around, playing her part perfectly. As if they had been lovers for years.

Without even blinking, John lowered his head but her hand came up and she pressed her fingers against his lips. "Don't mess up my lipstick." Her smile should be labeled lethal, because he totally believed the promise in her twinkling eyes as she let her gaze wander down his body and settle on his crotch. "Not until later."

Her husky pledge had his cock beginning to swell.

Anyone watching would believe they were completely engrossed in each other. He nipped at her finger. "Shit, Riss."

She laughed and hooked her arm through the crook of his, dragging him toward the front door. "Let's go meet our girl."

They'd picked the youngest-looking girl who they thought might be connected to Ortega based on Con's research. The plan was to get her alone, take pics of her, and then coerce her hopefully into talking. They also had the age-progression pictures of Sophia and Graciela. They wanted to see if their mark could identify either one of the girls. That decision was going to have to be made during the operation.

The double doors opened automatically, confirming that someone had indeed been watching their little show. A young Latino guy the size of a Hummer sat at the reception desk, dressed in a custom-made suit, expensive, and yet the peek of his holster was visible against a pristine white shirt. Here was the gatekeeper of the building. *And* the girls?

"Mr. and Mrs. Walker are here to see Anna," Rissa said haughtily, her head tilted so she was literally looking down her nose at the guy.

But that didn't seem to fluster him. He nodded at Rissa, his expression not betraying even a hint of annoyance.

"Guillermo will escort you." So they weren't allowed to wander by themselves. Interesting.

John reached for his wallet. "Can I...."

"Please sir." The guy's palm was the size of a dinner

plate as he held it up in the universal stop gesture. "Sign in here."

He handed John a clipboard with a waiver. Seriously? A freakin' waiver of responsibility.

Rissa pushed her sunglasses on top of her head to hold her hair back. Hopefully she'd activated the camera and gotten pics of the hulking security guard.

"But I wanted to pay now." John grinned, his gaze glued to Rissa. "We'll probably want to leave in a hurry."

John turned and winked at the guy, who didn't crack a smile.

The doorman narrowed his gaze. "I'd be happy to hold your wallet for you."

Before John could answer, the elevator doors slid open and the hulk's twin stepped out. These guys were jacked. "You need to leave your phones here."

"What?" They hadn't been expecting that. John opened his mouth to protest. *Stay in character.* He assumed most people would have an issue with leaving their phones. "I don't care for that."

"No pictures. No filming. No phones." The guy behind the desk spoke in a hard voice.

"We also have a strict no-weapon policy here." Their escort said, "I need to pat you down."

John stepped in front Rissa. "No one touches my wife." The rage that blossomed in his gut wasn't feigned. He did not want this guy touching Rissa.

"I'm sorry sir," the guy said without an ounce of remorse. John took note of the small ear bud in his ear. "If you want to go upstairs, then I need to check you for weapons."

"This is ridiculous," John blustered. Maybe they could get a line on the boss. "I want to talk to your manager."

"That is not possible." The guy stood in front of John hands held inches from his body. "May I check you?"

The guy behind the desk glanced at his watch, then nodded to the escort. Interesting, they must time the appointments so that clients didn't run into other clients.

John thought about stalling but he didn't want to call too much attention to them, and the cameras everywhere would be recording their images. John bet that came in handy if they had clients who got out of hand.

"It will be fine, sugar," Rissa cooed and curled her fingers around his forearm.

"Go ahead," he ground out.

The guy began his very efficient weapons check. He faltered when he hit John's prosthetic leg. Rather than put the guy on alert, John said tightly, "Car accident." His hair was long enough that it wasn't clear he was former military.

The guy nodded. "Thank you, sir. Ma'am."

Rissa took off her sunglasses and set them on the counter and spread her arms wide. John wanted to kiss her. He was pretty sure she'd aimed the camera at the guard's computer monitor. The angle wouldn't give them everything but it should at least capture some partial screenshots. "Frisk me, sugar."

Guillermo very efficiently skimmed his fingers over her body. John could feel his gorge rising. He hated that this thug had his hands on his woman. He clenched his fists and held back his anger.

Rissa smiled provocatively. "Well, sugar, I think we should be on a first-name basis after that little interlude." She ran a red-tipped nail over the guy's shoulder. "Are you on the menu?"

He flushed a bright crimson. "I can take you upstairs now."

The guard behind the desk held out his hand for their phones. John discreetly pressed a button to send a prearranged text to a burner to let Jack know they were on their way up to the room. Even though Jack was busy searching for the person threatening Shelley, he'd requested that John and Rissa keep him apprised of any developments.

"I'm locking my phone," John said, before handing it over to the guard even though if he tried to access it there wouldn't be any usable information on the device.

Rissa was already standing by the elevator. As the bell dinged, she said, "Oops." She had "forgotten" her sunglasses. She sauntered to the counter to grab them. "Very difficult to replace."

He could only hope that they might get some usable pictures. The camera had a WiFi connection and was transmitting the video to Con's laptop.

The guards waited impatiently for Rissa to get back to the elevator.

Within a minute, they were whisked up to the eighth floor. Guillermo knocked on the door brusquely. As soon as their appointment opened her door, the guard hustled back to the elevator. They had definitely thrown off the schedule.

The girl ushered them inside.

John and Rissa had already laid out what services they wanted when they'd made the appointment. Then they had discussed their plan in detail.

After they entered, John discreetly observed their surroundings.

The apartment was furnished with high-end antiques. And although the décor was somewhat impersonal, the room had the feel of an occupied space. It wasn't just a place to conduct business. She actually lived here.

"Hello, I am Anna." Her voice was cultured, low, melodic. She held out her hand. "Welcome to my home."

If John hadn't known that they had come here to pay for sex, he would have thought he was in a formal social setting. Her outfit was sexy without being too suggestive. The wrap dress would likely come off easily. He was pretty sure she was wearing garters and stockings underneath.

"It's a pleasure," Rissa purred, then lifted the girl's hand to her mouth and pressed a short kiss on the back. "To meet you."

John didn't let his surprise show, but it was difficult. He was used to covert in terms of slinking along the desert floor or stealth in movement, not this game of moves and counter moves.

They'd agreed that Rissa had more undercover experience and she should be the one to lead the mark. She sank languidly on to the sofa and pulled John with her.

Rissa squeezed John's hand three times.

Cameras.

Shit. So the girls, and their clients, were watched. John had to assume that not only were they being watched but that they were being taped.

Fuck.

The original plan was to take pictures of her and transmit them to an offsite location. Then John would inform her that unless she cooperated she would be arrested. Basically they were going to blackmail her to get her to talk.

Rissa's palm brushed over his shoulder. If he weren't so freaked out by the fact that there were cameras and this was going to have to go a lot further than he'd planned, he'd be amused at the fact that she was trying to comfort him.

They were going to have to shift their operation parameters.

John's body temp began to rise. He was going to have to let this…girl touch him.

While they'd discussed this contingency, knowing that he might have to get partially engaged with the girl in order to get her into a compromising position, he'd really hoped that this wouldn't happen.

Murphy's fucking law.

Anna sat gracefully in the chair across from them, spreading her legs just slightly, and it was clear she wasn't wearing underwear. Her neatly trimmed pubic hair was visible in the low light, the lighting set up to highlight her lack of undergarments.

She was gorgeous, all swarthy skin, big doe eyes, long thick lashes and an X-rated mouth. But he couldn't even garner a reaction. He was limp and flaccid. And to think he'd been more worried about getting a boner in front of his partner, and the woman he'd had sex with two nights ago. The thought of letting this girl—prisoner?—touch him made him want to throw up. But he needed to grow a pair.

Shit. They were going to have to work his lack of erection into their script.

"As you can see, my husband has…issues." Rissa cut an intense glance to his crotch. John wanted to laugh but he kept his expression stern.

"My wife—" he lifted her hand to his lips and ran his tongue over her palm "—likes to watch me with other women. It gets her off." He nipped the heel of her hand.

"So true, sugar."

"And that gets me off."

The girl nodded and stood. "Would you like to unwrap me?"

John swallowed his dismay. He could not let on that this situation was not what he wanted. "You do it."

She sauntered toward them on the sofa, her hips a sexy sway. He could tell she wasn't at all interested by the scene setting, she was acting. She clasped the tie that held her dress together, pulling it slightly so that the dress began to gape.

Sweat beaded at his hairline. The tie was completely undone. Her plum-colored dress gaped open and exposed her bare breasts, clearly surgically enhanced. They were ridiculously perky, and as she sauntered toward him, they didn't move. John couldn't help but compare them to Rissa's round pillowed form, a place to find comfort.

The girl let her dress slip off her shoulders and fall to the floor. She was clad in only a very skimpy lace garter the same color as the dress and old-fashioned stockings. The stockings nearly matched her skin tone. Clinically John analyzed her. Skin buffed and moisturized and slightly oiled, her pubic hair was tightly trimmed and landscaped.

The colors of both the dress and the undergarments were coordinated to complement the decorating. Did they use a freaking stager?

Anna slid her hands up to cup her fake breasts and squeezed her nipples, walking slowly, seductively toward them.

Except John couldn't even muster a semi in the girl's presence.

All he could think about was the cameras, and protecting Rissa. Which he knew was dumb. Rissa would take care of herself. Hopefully she was taking as many pictures as she could while the girl was focused on him.

Anna finally stood right in front of him. The heat from Rissa's body warmed his right side, but the rest of him was stone cold.

He took back his wish to work for Jack. If that made him

a pussy, then so be it but the thought of touching this…child was so far outside his comfort zone that he'd wandered into bizarro land.

Anna hesitated so briefly John might have thought he'd imagined it. But then she crawled over his lap, knees on either side of his hips, her position exactly like that of Rissa's the other night. Except then he'd been climbing out of his skin with need.

Now John's cock was still limp beneath his khakis.

"Seems as if he's going to need some more…enticing," Rissa said from beside him.

What the hell?

This scene was too close to the other night. The travesty of what he was about to do hit him in the gut. He was this close to lifting the girl off his lap and running for the door.

"He's shy." Rissa had injected a note of amusement in her voice, and right then he wanted to kill her. Not literally but when they were back at the suite, she was definitely going to get an earful.

Rissa covered his crotch with her hand, drawing his gaze from the girl whose tits were literally in his damn face. If she shifted the wrong way, she was going to put his eye out with her permanently pert nipples.

The familiar heat of Rissa's touch sparked his libido, and his dick, which had been very conspicuously limp, hardened in an instant.

John glared at Rissa and hoped the damn cameras couldn't see his expression or they thought they were having some sort of lover's spat.

"Let me do it, honey." Rissa tugged his zipper down while Anna rubbed her tits literally inches from his mouth. The scene should have been a guy's fantasy—two women, there for his enjoyment. Instead, he just wanted out.

This was awkward as hell.

Rissa's scent drifted toward him and his dick started to rise as she lightly caressed him through his cotton briefs.

He was not going to have sex with this girl. He wondered if there were cameras in the bathroom. Maybe he could take her in there and they could continue on with their plan.

"I've got it." Anna decided to assert herself.

She leaned over and pulled his cock out. Rissa had to move, otherwise she would have gotten a face full of Anna's breasts.

The girl wrapped her cool hand around John's dick and tugged. He immediately went limp again.

Before he could make up some stupid excuse, there was a loud banging at the door. "Police. Open up."

"What?" John practically jumped up from the sofa. "Shit."

What the hell was going on? The cops were here?

"What is happening?" Anna stood there, naked as a jay except for the garter, stockings, and high heels, a bewildered expression on her face. Her gaze shot to the camera strategically aimed at the sofa.

The door flew open.

And everyone froze.

Anna clapped her arm over her breasts.

John lifted his hands in the air. He hadn't survived four tours with the Marines in order to get shot in an upscale bordello by the LVPD. His pants gaped open, his dick hanging in the wind, although hopefully the tails of his button-down shirt covered him up.

Next to him, Rissa glared haughtily at the cops, her expression the perfect mimicking of a wealthy woman who thought she was above the law.

John only dimly listened to the cops mirandizing Anna. She shook violently, appearing terrified and completely out of her element.

"John Walker." The uniformed office placed his arms behind his back.

"Now see here, I think there's been some sort of mistake."

"I don't think so, *sir*," the cop sneered.

John knew he had to play the part. But he damn well hoped he could get these charges dropped. "At least let me zip up my pants."

The officer shook his head curtly. "No can do." The officer cuffed his hands behind his back. "You are under arrest for the solicitation of prostitution."

"Don't you think we could…work something out here?" John cajoled. Trying desperately to bribe the damn cop. Just like Mr. Walker would do if he was actually Mr. Walker.

"No, sir." The tone was just a little bit more snide.

John hung his head.

Meanwhile, the cops had gotten Anna some clothes and she stood meekly, an expression of complete terror on her face.

He'd have to guess that getting arrested wouldn't go well for her once she was out. Shit.

"Can you at least zip my pants for me?"

"This is unacceptable," Rissa said haughtily. "I have done nothing wrong. Why are you doing this to me?"

"You're going to have to come along and give a statement, ma'am."

"Are these handcuffs really necessary?" she whined. Then she shifted her approach and started to flirt with the cop. "I suppose under the right circumstances they could be fun."

Rage began to burn underneath his breastbone, pulsing in a relentless ache. He knew she was just playing her part. He knew it. But still. "Shut up, Rissa."

"You shut up." Rissa gave him a disdainful look. "If you didn't have problems getting it up, then we wouldn't be in this mess."

The cops behind him snickered. And John suppressed a laugh. But he was only partially amused, because if Jack didn't come through on the one phone call, they were screwed.

CHAPTER 11

Rissa opened the door to the suite and trudged to a stool at the breakfast bar. God, she really wanted a shower. Spending the past seven hours at the police station was not her idea of a good time.

The door slammed as John stalked in behind her. He was pissed. He had pretty much steamed silently beside her the whole way home, like the volcano getting ready to erupt at The Mirage. Everyone knew it was coming.

If Jack's cop friend hadn't kept up a running banter, discussing where they would go next in this case, then Rissa was sure that John would have been yelling at her.

She had no clue why.

Could she help it if she was the tiniest bit pleased that he hadn't been able to get an erection even with the totally gorgeous, skinny young girl nearly naked and in his lap? It wasn't lost on her that the girl had been in the exact same position as Rissa two nights ago.

So that wasn't the problem.

As soon as Rissa put her hand on his zipper, he'd gotten hard.

And that fact thrilled her down to her very bones.

Now the only thing she was particularly happy about was that Maria wouldn't be able to hear when this fight started.

After they'd been arrested, they'd called Jack. Except he'd been in the middle of dealing with the capture of Shelley's stalker, so he'd palmed them off on Jack's LVPD buddy.

Thankfully Keisha and Shane were in town for the wedding. The GHR employee and the freelance pilot were now a couple. Keisha had taken Maria under her wing when the whole confrontation with José Fernandez went down. So when they knew they wouldn't be back for hours, John had asked Keisha to pick up Maria and bring her back to the Palazzo.

John wrenched open a kitchen cabinet door and plucked out a glass. With his teeth he tugged out the cork in the scotch bottle, spit it onto the counter and then poured and poured and poured until the glass was full to the brim.

He held the glass in his hand, the other balled into a fist and propped on his hip while he stared blindly at the microwave over the stovetop.

He slugged down half the glass, then prowled toward her. She shouldn't be turned on, but damn he was a study in hard angles and pissed-off alpha male. His shirt was partway unbuttoned, revealing the fuzz of chest hair that she personally knew led in a happy trail straight down to his impressive erection.

"What. The. Hell?"

That was all he growled. His hazel eyes glowed with an unholy light. His lips were sheened with the remnants of the scotch. Rissa inhaled deeply taking his essence in as if she could taste him.

Her panties went damp. Primal. Prey. She was in his sights and she loved it.

"We had to make it look good." She kept her voice steady but it was difficult. All she wanted to do was lean forward and unzip his pants and devour him.

He jerked her to her feet. Rissa slammed against his chest. John wrapped his arm around her back, fisted her hair in his meaty grip, and yanked her head back. He exhaled scotch breath against her lips.

"We didn't have to go that far." John was breathing hard, his chest expanding and contracting against her breasts. "I was going to protest the cameras. Find a way to get us out of there."

"Not as effective," Rissa countered. God, his erection was prodding her in the belly, her knees were this close to going weak, and all she wanted was him inside her.

The adrenaline rush from being undercover, improvising, even the cops barging in, banged through her in a flood of endorphins.

Could he tell that she was on the edge?

Rissa gave in to her lust and kissed him. She ate at his mouth, tasting the sweet, smoky flavor of his drink before he broke away from her kiss. "You handled it." *Please, please handle me.*

"You handled me." John nipped the shell of her ear.

Shivers cascaded over her spine. And she wanted to handle him again. This time with her mouth.

She dragged her hands up his chest and fisted his hair just as tightly. He was as hot as she was, even if he didn't want to be.

Rissa scraped her teeth along his throat and sucked at the hollow at perfect mouth level. She rubbed against him, his cock hardening even further, and Jesus, she wanted him inside her. Now.

Needed him to fill that aching, lonely place.

He jerked up her dress and pulled down her panties, her bare ass hanging in the cool air of the hotel room. His hot, thick fingers skimmed over her ass and delved into her weeping pussy.

Rissa fumbled with his pants. Wanting to do the same to him. Bare his ass and cock for her touching pleasure.

He held her so tightly she could barely breathe and she didn't care. Breathing was overrated.

Pleasure cascaded through her, and fireworks detonated behind her closed eyes as his rough fingers caressed her. He dragged his fingers through her folds, coating them with her arousal. She was drenched. So wet that his fingers slid right in.

God she was so close to coming all over his hand.

Rissa moaned against his throat. So hard to concentrate. She pulled down his zipper and reached into his briefs, just like she'd done earlier today. Except now, for her, he was as hard as the club the cop had used to nudge them into the squad car. She curled her fingers around his fat, smooth pole and rubbed the tip of her thumb over his head. Moisture coated her hand and she knew he was as on edge as she was.

She shoved his khakis down until they were around his thighs, and gripped his ass. They rocked against each other as the frenzy inside built to a deafening fever pitch.

She nipped her way along his strong jaw until she hit his earlobe. "Please." *Fuck me.*

She was begging and she didn't care.

Their position was too awkward to move from, especially with John's pants constricting his movements.

"I need you inside me," she demanded. "Now."

"Fuck, Rissa."

A visceral thrill raced through her as he groaned her name. Her sex was a gaping, empty vessel that only he could fill. They needed to stay right here and slake their thirst. Her brain desperately searched for a way to make this happen. Now.

John took a careful step back. "No," she moaned.

But then he spun her around so she faced the barstool she'd been perched on. With rough, impatient hands he grabbed her hips.

"Yes." Rissa figured out what he wanted and bent over, stuck her ass in the air, giving him access. "Do it."

She hated that she couldn't see his face, but when his fat head rubbed at her pussy all thoughts disappeared into a puff of lust.

Her sex clenched, trying to suck his cock inside her by sheer force of will.

"Stop being so gentle. Fuck me," she commanded.

John slammed inside.

God, he filled her up. His thick staff invaded, conquered, and her body surrendered like a maiden to a marauding Viking.

He dominated, shoving into her with sharp, short thrusts. Every slam of their bodies hit that spot inside her and supercharged her pleasure. Rissa gripped the edge of the seat and rammed back against his thrusts as he pounded into her.

Her ass slammed against his belly, his balls slapped against her pussy with each bang.

The rest of her body was still completely covered. The cushioned seat of the barstool abraded her tight nipples.

And even with her heels on she had to stand on her tiptoes for the perfect angle.

John grunted with every rock and thrust of his hips. Pressure built inside her until she exploded in a fiery mass. White lights sparkled behind her closed eyelids as her body imploded in a spectacular concussion of sound and sensation.

Euphoria fizzed in her bloodstream, the culmination of all those lovely pheromones. Rissa sagged against the seat of the barstool. She rested her cheek on the cushion, her chest heaving and her breath coming in quick pants.

Still buried deep inside her, the root of John's cock pressed relentlessly against her clit. He jerked as he came, brutal jets shot inside her, his orgasm pulsing vigorously against her sensitized channel. He continued to pump into her, and another climax rolled over her.

She had never come so intensely in her life. A swell of gratitude and thick strong emotion crowded her, making it difficult to breathe.

Out of her peripheral vision she watched him stiffen. Remorse and revulsion stole over him. She knew he was going to pull away a moment before he withdrew from her body.

Sticky semen trickled down her leg, like the hope and gratitude trickling from her heart. Until another more practical thought entered her mind. They'd had unprotected sex.

She was on the pill. But still, not the brightest move.

She lay there, not wanting to face him. Not wanting to see the loathing in his eyes. He'd been pissed. Not horny. And still she didn't necessarily want to see the condemnation on his face. Not wanting to be hit with what was sure to be an emotional blow.

She knew he'd never hit her physically. But words could damage more easily than tissue and bones.

"Fuck me." He stumbled away from her and put his hand out to steady himself on the breakfast bar counter.

She refused to play the wounded victim. "I believe those were my words."

John flinched.

Rissa pulled up her thong and pulled down her dress. She could cover her body far more efficiently than she could protect her heart.

But slowly she stood and faced him.

His pants hovered at mid-thigh. His cock was still semi-erect and glistened with her juices in the low light of the kitchen.

The evidence of their mistake and their passion was enough to have her knees dip. He was gorgeous.

But that wasn't going to get her out of this sudden awkwardness.

"Nothing like angry sex to take the edge off." Rather than pretend that hadn't just happened, she was going to shove it in his face. Show him that she was fine. That she wasn't figuratively shattered and lying naked on the cool ceramic tile.

She'd deal with the fallout, no problem.

Holy shit. He'd practically mauled her. John yanked his pants to his waist, he needed to get the fuck away from her.

Her words, *angry sex*, rolled through him in a tide of shame.

"Good to know you're DTF with a cripple to take the edge off." He hoped the crude sentiment would have her run. But he should have known better.

"You've got to admit, you needed it." She'd angled

slightly away from him, so he couldn't see her face. See her eyes.

You needed it. But she had too. Unless…had that really been what happened just now? She'd taken pity on him? It certainly hadn't seemed that way, but shit. His perceptions of life were skewed, weren't they? All his life he'd believed his father was a hero. Then he'd found out the guy was a class-A asshole.

Maybe his entire life had been some kind of disconnect between his wishes and reality.

Because how else could he explain what had just happened? Yes, he'd been pissed.

She'd put herself in harm's way. And he'd had no fucking idea how to get them out of the situation. Until the very end of their night, when Jack's pal from Vice came into the interrogation room, he'd really thought they were going to jail. At the very least for the night.

But it turned out their entire booking was for show. The cops had gone through the arrest processes so that whoever was running the stable of prostitutes wouldn't get suspicious of them.

According to Jack's friend at the LVPD, they had been trying for years to get something on this ring but couldn't ever get anyone to roll over on who was running the building. Once the Feds had been made aware that the entire building was basically one big bordello, they had someone on site at the LVPD in a matter of hours.

And finally with the information that Jack had given them regarding Manuel Ortega, they were able to reverse trace ownership of the building back to Ortega.

It was a major break in their case.

John and Rissa had gotten a break too. Anna had not identified either Sophia or Graciela, but her heart rate and temperature had elevated at their pictures, so they now knew that she knew, or had known, them.

Anna was currently in protective custody. They didn't want Ortega to be tipped off.

They were preparing the warrants but because of the scope of the search and arrest, it was going to take a few days to get all their ducks in a row. In the meantime, John and Rissa were supposed to sit tight. But John had no intention of waiting to find Sophia and Graciela.

No matter what the FBI and the LVPD wanted.

"What are you thinking right now?" She narrowed her eyes at him.

"Forget it." John jerked on his zipper and let the tails of his shirt cover the damp material of his crotch.

"But—"

"Tomorrow I'll continue the search for the girls." John didn't need or want her help.

"You don't…trust me." Rissa jammed her hands on her hips, the action strained the material of her top.

John's dick started to rise at the covered mounds. How was it even possible that he could get turned on by a tight little dress that covered Rissa, when Anna's bare breasts, right in his face, had done nothing? That pissed him off even more. His body reacted to Rissa's without any effort on her part, which was why he needed to get the fuck away from her.

"Sure I do." He shifted his gaze away from her. Away from the temptation. Because as much as he liked her, she didn't want him for anything other than a quick fuck in the dark.

"Really?"

"But you can stay here and guard Maria," John said. "It's going to be hard enough for her as it is, once she finds out that her friends have been basically prisoners all these years."

Rissa had a pained expression on her face. "We can have Maria stay with Keisha and Shane. Then we can both look for the girls."

"I'd rather handle this part of the operation by myself." John shook his head. "One person will be less conspicuous than two."

They had a very limited window of opportunity. The LVPD could only "hold" Anna for seventy-two hours before they had to release her or charge her. If they didn't, then Ortega would definitely get suspicious.

Because the doorman refused to take money, the case against Anna was nearly nonexistent, even though she was naked when the cops burst in. There was no evidence to support the solicitation charge, even with Nevada's loose interpretation of solicitation.

Rissa snarled, "Well, that isn't very partner-like."

John retreated a step.

A sharp, stabbing sensation transformed his left quad muscle into an instrument of pain.

He must have made some sound because Rissa's annoyance shifted to concern. "What's wrong?"

"Nothing." He held the groan in his chest and tried to breathe through the excruciating cramp as his muscle bunched into a hard knot and gripped so tight he wondered if he'd ever loosen up again.

Just like his yoga instructor had taught him, he envisioned sending healing breath to the ravaged muscle so it would relax.

Bile rose in his stomach.

"Not nothing." She fisted her hands on her hips, waiting for his answer.

"Cramp," he ground out harshly. God, his leg was on fire. "I'm fine."

She snorted. "Right."

"I will be in a minute," he clarified. He was lying through his clenched teeth.

"Bet if I count to sixty, you'll still be in pain."

"See you in the morning." He hoped she'd just go quietly to her room. At the very least the after-sex awkward was gone, replaced by story-of-his-life awkward. And yeah if he had a little pang of regret, he'd squash it.

John didn't want to pivot around. His good leg could handle it but he wasn't sure the shift in balance would work for his left.

Piercing pain stabbed through his leg, traveling up his hamstring and zinging his lower back as he backed away slowly.

"How can I help?" Rissa grabbed his forearm lightly.

She couldn't. No one could. He just needed to get to his bed, and fall back in agony, until the cramps went away. "I'll be fine."

John swallowed a sigh of relief when she headed to her room.

He should have thought more about his leg earlier. Today had been much longer than a typical day for him. When he went to work for Jack, he'd have to pay more attention to what was going on with his body.

John limped carefully toward his bed, trying to put as little weight as possible on his fully knotted-up leg.

If he could get there and get his prosthetic off, he'd start to feel better. That was his story and he was sticking to it. If sheer determination counted, he'd definitely feel better soon. Hopefully.

His heartbeat thudded in his ears as the wash of pain

drowned out everything else. John dropped to his
king-size bed.

He closed his eyes and groaned. This was going to hurt
like a bitch.

Next to him the bed depressed. His eyes popped open
and there she was, holding a large glass of water in her
hand.

"Drink this."

He gulped down the water in one long swallow and
shoved the glass back at her. Rissa set the glass on the half
wall that separated the Jacuzzi tub from the bedroom area.

But she still didn't leave.

John figured there was one way to make her leave. His
stomach heaved as he unzipped his pants and shoved them
halfway down his thighs. It wasn't lost on him that right this
moment his pants were in the exact same spot as when he'd
been pounding into her from behind. An easy way to avoid
the reality of having sex with an amputee.

She pushed him back on the bed. "Lift your hips."

The pressure on his leg sent fiery shooting pains
through his body but he bit back a moan and lifted up.
Rissa eased his khakis down his legs. She knelt at his feet to
gently remove his shoes and then slid his pants all the
way off.

John curled to an upright position and began the process
of taking off his prosthetic. Fuck, the pump to remove the
suction seal was on the other side of the bed.

John rubbed his hands down his face and let his breath
out in a heavy sigh. "Can you hand me that pump on the
bedtable?"

She retrieved the pump and handed it to him silently.

"I'm good now." But she still didn't leave.

John began the process of removing his leg, bile roiled in

his stomach. This time from an odd kind of fear, rather than pain.

With the exception of that moment in the tub, no one besides his doctors and nurses had ever seen his stump in the light. Yeah, he knew he needed to get over it. But recovery was a slow, one-step-forward, two-steps-backward process. And dealing with someone else's disgust was pretty far down on his list of problems.

He rolled off the silicone liner that protected his residual limb. John had a myoelectric prosthetic that registered electrical impulses from his body and helped with ankle mobility. Although typically more common in arm prosthesis, it worked in his transtibial limb. He finished removing his limb and tossed it on the bed.

Rissa chuckled. "Semper Fi." The cover for his limb was tattooed with the Marine Corps motto and shield.

"Ooh rah," John said wryly.

Once the pressure on his stump eased, the muscles of his quad and thigh knotted even more tightly. As if the muscle had been waiting for him to release the suction hold and torture him.

Peppermint, crisp and energizing, permeated the room. Suddenly Rissa placed her warm, oiled hands over the tense muscles. With deep digs of her thumbs she massaged in circular motions, spending most of her time on the giant knot at mid-thigh.

"I'll smell like a fucking candy cane."

"But you'll feel much better," she argued.

John opened his mouth to grouse some more, but she was right. The peppermint oil had already began heating and warming his muscles, and the knot was slowly dissipating.

She continued up and down the length of his thigh, at

one point coming way too close to his crotch. And like Pavlov's dogs, as soon as her fingers hit a certain point, his dick rose up to show its appreciation of her efforts.

He thought about ignoring his body's response. "He likes you."

"I like him too," she finally replied. She tilted her head so that her hair hid her face. "Is it okay if I…?"

She gestured to his stump.

Based on the way the rest of his leg was feeling, he thought it might help. But then she'd have to touch it. He actually avoided looking at the severed limb even though he still rubbed the damaged tissue daily to help with nerve endings and scar tissue.

"Yeah." When she put her hands on him, he moaned.

"It must really hurt," she murmured.

His mouth quirked. "It's just a papercut."

"Excuse me?"

"That's what the multiple amputees call my injury."

Rissa's melodic laughter wrapped him in joy. "Really?"

"Yeah." Those guys made his simple amputation easier to bear.

"Roll over."

"Someone is bossy."

"Always." She nudged him. So John finally rolled over onto his stomach. And Rissa began to massage his hamstring. He hadn't even appreciated how tight he was until she hit a particularly sore spot and dug in.

Rissa had climbed up on the bed and was perched next to him as she worked at the tense muscles beneath her fingers.

The heat from her oil-warmed hands was working on other parts of his anatomy in unsuspecting ways. His erection pressed into the mattress, and he stifled a groan that wasn't entirely due to the release of tension in his muscles. As she continued, his cock hardened even more.

The room heated, shrank, until breath stopped up in his lungs because the tenor of her massage had changed from therapeutic to long, slow meandering strokes that detonated his brain, synapses firing in a completely inappropriate manner.

Hadn't they decided the hate fuck from earlier had been a mistake?

Warm peppermint vanquished the last of the stink from the police station. "As nice as this has been…" He began the simple words to get her out of his room. And the fuck off his bed, before they did something they'd regret. Again.

Rissa straddled his thighs, pushed the tails of his button-down shirt up until she could pull the shirt over his head, exposing his bare back. She rubbed her hands over him in long, leisurely strokes. She bent over his back, pressing harder until he could feel her breath on the back of his neck.

"Nice?" She nipped at his shoulder blade, hard enough to sting.

Yeah, not a very exciting commentary. He'd done it on purpose to try to get her out of here.

He cleared his throat.

The good news was he'd forgotten all about his leg. The bad, he was never going to recover from the boner currently prodding the mattress as if it could burrow inside.

"It's been a long day," he tried again, almost desperately.

She nodded her agreement but ignored the implicit message and pressed openmouthed kisses up the center of his back, then veered toward his right shoulder. She licked his neck as her hands smoothed over his triceps and down his forearms.

And finally John surrendered. He closed his eyes on an exhale and let her tend to his body. Because that's what she was doing. Tending to him. Soothing, even as she aroused.

With an easy flop, she lay on top of him. Her generous breasts flattened into his deltoids, her belly rested on the curve of his ass, and she nuzzled her head into the valley between his shoulder blades.

The puff of her breath along his skin peppered goosebumps over his entire body.

He wanted. Ached. Longed to flip over and devour her. She continued to smooth her palms over his skin. Her lashes fluttered against his back.

"Are you…falling asleep?" He couldn't say why but that amused him. And pleased him.

That she was comfortable enough to let herself go, to trust him enough to sleep in his presence, on top of him, caused a warmth to pool in his belly and spread out in waves.

Her breathing deepened, and her body melted over his.

The more boneless she became, the harder it was for him to draw breath. His chest was tight with emotions he didn't know how to process. There was something far more intimate about falling asleep together rather than the screaming orgasms they'd had in the living room. Her absolute trust was a gift.

Instead of reaching around and pushing her off his body and forcing her to back to her own room, John settled into the mattress and let out a puff of breath. The world tilted on its access, throwing him more off balance than when he was using his crutches. Because right now he had no desire to send her away.

He liked the way she felt on top of him, surrounding him. A curious sense of anticipation and hope flooded him.

The emotion filled his chest, and he decided to savor the embrace rather than push her away. She'd wake up in a second and everything would be back to normal.

She'd be her bitchy self.

He'd be his grumpy, untouchable self.

CHAPTER 12

Rissa stepped from the shower and wrapped a towel around her wet hair.

She'd woken up in bed with John. In. Bed.

She didn't remember falling asleep. She'd been stroking his gorgeous back and arms, trying to soothe him.

She wasn't a soothing person. And yet, in that moment, she'd wanted to take care of him. She'd known that he was self-conscious about her seeing his stump. But she didn't care about that. In that moment, she'd felt a closeness, a kinship with him that defied reason.

They barely knew each other. And yet, his soul called to hers.

She understood him. She liked him. She admired him.

And the sex.

She sighed. The sex was phenomenal.

Someone knocked at the door to the suite. Rissa headed for the door. Through the open doorway to John's room, he lay tangled in the bedspread, half on his stomach and his bare arms curled around a pillow like a lover.

Her heart thudded, hard, at the display of all that

power. Even in sleep he dominated the space with his commanding masculine presence. She'd had the full force of his attention focused on her last night. Heat seared through her veins. Too bad most of the time they butted heads.

The knock came again.

Probably Jack bringing back Maria. Dammit. It had been so late last night. And she and John had argued. She should have let Jack know right away that she wanted to go with John to search for the girls rather than babysit Maria.

She glanced through the peephole but all she could see was the back of a dark head of hair. With one last longing glance back at John, Rissa yanked open the door.

Shit. It wasn't Jack.

The barrel of a cannon was aimed at her heart. She couldn't hear, could only react to the sight of that weapon. Her damn nemesis. Guaranteed to make her tremble, and not in the good way. Her heart thumped loudly, as if her veins had shriveled in fear and blood banged against the walls in a primal drumbeat. Frantic to push through and send nourishment to her heart.

She could only pray that John stayed very still. Maybe the dark-haired giant holding her hostage wouldn't notice him.

"Ms. Evans."

There's no sense in denying I'm me. Based on the surety with which he's holding the weapon, if I said no, I'm not sure he won't shoot.

Rissa didn't take her gaze from his gun as he pushed his way inside. He lumbered slowly, his size clearly an impediment. And as she backed into the room, she thought between John and her, they might be able to take him.

Except behind him there was an equally behemoth man.

With an equally behemoth gun.

Fuck. It was happening again.

She could hear John rustling. Even though the man had spoken in a low voice, it had clearly registered with John.

Big Guy number one jerked his head toward the bedroom.

Big Guy number two halted in John's bedroom doorway. "Don't move."

Out of her peripheral vision she could see John. He had his limb in his hand. "Shit, this one's a cripple," the asshole said.

"He's also a former Marine, you dickhead," Big Guy number one snarled. "Don't let him put the leg on."

Shit.

"Get up slowly." Big Guy number two tossed John's basketball shorts at him. "And get dressed."

"Clearly you have us at a disadvantage," she said pleasantly. They knew their names and the fact that John used to be a Marine. "Who are you?"

The only potential ace in their hand was the fact that Jack could be on his way. Except he wouldn't be expecting an ambush.

"Doesn't matter who we are," Big Guy number one growled. "You're coming with us."

With efficient movements they rounded up John and Rissa. One aimed their weapon at them while the other zip-tied Rissa's wrists behind her back. They let John have his hands free to use one crutch. They made him leave the other behind.

They were clearly professionals because both men stayed out of reach. Big Guy number two stayed out of crutch reach of John. And Big Guy number one stayed out of kick reach of Rissa. The response time to pull the trigger would protect the big guys if John and Rissa tried to rush either one of them.

All she could do was thank the Universe that Maria had spent the night at the Palazzo. What if she'd been here? She was slowly regaining her confidence but getting kidnapped again could have totally set her back.

Small favors.

Rissa and John could really use a big favor right now.

Within two minutes, they were out the door. The two men followed, weapons discreetly tucked against their sides. There was no room for escape.

John awkwardly swung his crutch trying to keep his balance without his prosthetic, his mouth set in a grim line. She'd bet he was thinking the same thing she was. They were screwed.

Fuck. John pretty much couldn't come up with anything more than that one word.

The fucking goons had the tactical advantage right now. Because without his leg his mobility was extremely limited.

And Rissa was flat-out terrified of the gun.

This situation was her worst nightmare come back to haunt her.

"You okay?" he murmured.

She swallowed. "Yeah."

"Shut up," Goon One snarled.

John tightened his fingers on the handle of his crutch. He'd managed to send a quick SOS text to Jack while he was still in bed. But since John and Rissa's phones were back in the hotel room, that basically just let Jack know they hadn't disappeared of their own free will. He needed to get his brain in gear and figure out how the hell they were going to get out of this.

But forty minutes later, he was still grasping for a solution.

They had loaded John and Rissa into a shiny black three-row Cadillac Escalade. They were in the far back. The driver, Goon Two, stayed well within the speed limit while Goon One, definitely the smarter one, kept his weapon trained on them during the ride out into the desert.

Pretty much everything about this situation sucked.

The goons hadn't disguised their faces. They hadn't covered John and Rissa's eyes for the ride. Which meant they didn't care if John and Rissa could identify them and exactly where they went. Which presumably meant they didn't intend for them to get out of this alive.

Fuck if he'd survive an IED during a wartime situation only to buy it in a Las Vegas desert.

There was fucking nothing out in the desert. Hills and scrub and rocks, until the SUV pulled to a stop in front of what appeared to be an abandoned mine shaft. Signs warning of danger were posted all around, but the area was empty except for one other car. A beat-up old Honda Civic.

The two goons gestured for them to get out of the car but stayed far enough back that there was no way to rush them without getting shot. "Wait for a distraction," John murmured.

Although what that was going to be, John had no fucking clue.

They led them toward a boarded-up entrance to the mine. Dust kicked up as John dragged his crutch through the sand leaving a trail.

When they got close enough, John could see that the boards had been tampered with.

Rissa was shaking with anxiety. He wasn't sure how much longer she'd last.

Goon Two forced them into the mine shaft. And there was Ortega. John recognized the man from the pictures Jack had shared. Ortega was dressed in a lightweight tan suit and tie with a dapper straw fedora resting on a cap of black curls. His nearly black eyes assessed them shrewdly.

"Well, Mr. Pulaski. Ms. Evans. Nice to make your acquaintance." He smiled, a blatant show of teeth and rage.

John nodded.

Rissa didn't say a word. She was too busy checking out the two lumps in the corner. Her eyes had taken on a shiny glossiness and her body transformed before his eyes. The shaking, the fear had melted away as soon as she'd seen those lumps.

Fascinating. She hadn't been upset about her own safety. But if John were correct, they had just found Sophia and Graciela. And Rissa had found her courage.

"And you are?" Rissa asked coolly.

"Not important." But he said it with such hubris that John wanted to punch the guy.

"On the contrary, Señor Ortega." John tried to rattle him. "You're the man we've been looking for."

Ortega squinted. That didn't make him happy. John goaded him some more. "You're into some naughty things."

"*Suficiente.*" Ortega shut him up with a slash of his hand. "Tell me how you knew to look for me. Tell me how you knew to look for these women."

He gave a chin lift toward the lumps.

John zipped through options. He could really use Rissa's FBI experience right now. Ortega knew John was a Marine but there was absolutely nothing to tie him to Jack anywhere in any system. Not yet. For which John could be thankful.

But since Ortega knew Rissa's real name, he figured it wouldn't be long before Ortega tied Rissa to Bliss and then Maria. Then the logical leap to Fernandez.

They both stayed silent. No way would he give up Maria.

And that's when John figured out that Rissa was using her FBI experience. She was trying to get Ortega to give up information.

"Why did an unemployed former Marine and an employee of Elite Image Management join together to find these girls?"

John kept his face impassive. But inside he was *What the Fuck-ing* all over the place.

So Adams-Larsen gave their actual employees covers? With a small sigh of relief, he figured out that Ortega wasn't going to be able to tie either of them to the Stone family. Which meant that even if they didn't make it out alive, this *pendejo* was going down.

Rissa had given him a tiny head nod toward her wrists. He hoped she was telling him that she could break the zip cuffs. It was possible if you knew what you were doing.

That was his woman.

His. Woman. Damn, but he liked that.

Goon One had stepped outside, presumably to guard the entrance. So they were down to Goon Two and Ortega in the mine shaft. If they could disarm Goon Two before Goon One made it inside, they might have a chance. Two against three weren't great odds. But fuck it, Rissa kept staring at those lumps, and he knew she'd handle it. Handle this.

"What made you connect me to *these* girls?" Ortega was starting to get rattled at their continued silence. He had moved closer to the women, who cowered against the filthy, crumbling wall of the abandoned mine. In the dim light, John couldn't see their faces. But based on Ortega's question, he hoped they were Sophia and Graciela.

John wondered how Ortega knew they'd been trying to find Sophia and Graciela.

Their continued insubordination was starting to have an impact. A small dollop of spittle lingered in the corner of Ortega's mouth. Although it was a legitimate question. The only people who had questioned Anna about the girls were the LVPD.

So how *did* he know that John and Rissa were specifically looking for Sophia and Graciela? They couldn't ask.

"Why do *you* think we're looking for them?" Rissa finally spoke.

"Answer my question."

"You stole them from their families." Rissa accused.

"I gave them a life free from the dirty fields, laboring in the hot sun for less than minimum wage, forced to shit in the outhouses and sleep in hovels."

"How'd you do it?" Rissa taunted. "Get them hooked on drugs?"

"Of course not. I've seen how that garbage ravages the body. My girls are clean."

"Something to be super proud of," Rissa sneered.

"Instead of filth and squalor, they live in luxury. They wear designer clothing. These shoes," Ortega wrenched the leg of one of the women to show them the red sole of the shiny patent leather pump, "cost six hundred dollars on sale. That dress is a designer original. Last season, but still."

John used the moment to swing closer to the two terrified women, pretending to try to see their shoes and clothes. Ortega didn't seem to notice because he was hyper focused on Rissa and justifying his actions.

"So pretty clothes make up for being stolen from their families?"

Ortega lifted the girl's trembling hand to smell her skin. "She bathes in the fragrance of Chanel No. 5. No cheap homemade concoction that dries the skin and husks the body."

"They're slaves," Rissa spat. "How do you live with yourself?"

"My mama would have killed to live like this."

"You're a fucking monster."

"I'm not a monster." And John could see that Ortega truly believed that. "I'm their savior."

"So they could leave any time they want?"

He cracked a laugh.

"I gave them this life. And I can take it away." A mean look entered his deep brown gaze. "But they don't want to leave."

"They *can't* leave." Rissa taunted him again. "You're nothing but a thief and a pimp."

With every taunt she'd moved farther away from the girls and toward Goon Two at the doorway.

But her accusation sent Ortega into a rage and he stalked toward Rissa, who was now only a few feet away from the entrance.

Goon Two was trying to keep track of Rissa and John but his gaze naturally kept returning to Riss. *Divide and conquer, baby.*

God, John wanted to jump into the fray. His entire body itched with the need to take these fuckers down. He wanted to be the one to save the day and take out their captors but his mobility was seriously compromised without his prosthetic and only one crutch. His goal was to get the girls out of the line of fire. And trust Rissa to take care of the others.

He was just waiting for the right distraction.

RISSA KNEW she had to get Ortega just a little further away from the girls. "You're a common criminal."

"*Silencio!*" Ortega roared and backhanded Rissa.

Luckily Rissa had seen the hit coming.

She dodged the worst of the blow and dropped down perfectly, slamming her arms against the pebbled stone floor. The flex cuffs snapped.

Her sudden movement and Ortega's yell startled the bats clinging to the ceiling. With a loud squeal they descended.

The bats created the perfect diversion. Ortega had covered his head with his arms and was ducking down. Not paying any attention to Rissa or John. The women huddled against the cave wall were screaming.

For a moment, Rissa panicked. Her blood pounded a frantic rhythm pulsing at her brain. What if she failed?

What if she froze?

She knew John was waiting for her signal. She nodded and he swung his crutch at Ortega, just as Rissa swung her legs at the guy guarding the cave entrance in a classic takedown maneuver.

Thank you, Kita. The next time she saw her fellow Adams-Larsen coworker, she was going to give her a great big hug for insisting that even the receptionist needed to know some moves.

Ortega was out cold on the dirt floor.

Big Guy number two went down at the same time Ortega did. And in a stroke of amazing good luck, he hit his head and he was out.

Unfortunately, in a stroke of amazing bad luck, the idiot discharged his weapon. The bang was loud in the disturbed air. And the bats went even crazier.

Rissa didn't have time to worry about John. She grabbed the thug's weapon, knowing she only had a few seconds before Big Guy number one came barreling through the entrance. Rissa pushed up against the wall and waited. She held the .357 in both hands, the grip far too big for her. Her arms shook, but she didn't lower the weapon. Couldn't.

She was pretty sure she'd seen a stain of blood on the floor near John but she couldn't take the chance of taking her attention away from the entrance.

She'd only have seconds.

Big Guy number one was smart. He didn't come rushing into the mine shaft. He moved cautiously but he was still dealing with his eyes adjusting to the dark interior when he came through the doorway. He held his weapon out, ready to fire. And she knew she had no choice.

Rissa's breath caught. Bile rose, like it had at the range the other day. Her arms shook and tears pooled in her eyes.

She had to trust that John was taking care of the two women. Getting them out of harm's way.

And as the guy came fully into the chamber, she knew she had to protect those women. They deserved everything. With a trembling finger, she aimed square at his chest. She breathed in jerkily.

Then exhaled and pulled the trigger.

The suite was overrun with people.

Jack and Bliss were there. Connor and Ava. Shelley and Ric. Colin and Jess. Rissa's boss Jillian Larsen had already been on her way to Vegas. She'd arrived right when all hell had broken loose. Rissa hadn't had a chance to thank Jill for having the confidence in her that she hadn't had in herself.

"Nice job." Jack lifted his glass and toasted John and Rissa.

Rissa's gaze shot to John. They literally hadn't been alone since everything happened. She had some questions. The most important one was what the hell had he been thinking? But that would have to wait until they were alone.

Bliss smiled happily. "To John and Rissa."

John and Rissa.

She liked the way that sounded way too much.

John lifted his glass of Johnny Walker Black and clinked it against his brother's. Rissa ignored her glass and set it on the counter.

Ava's smile was bittersweet—which Marissa understood

well. The arrests had brought about the answers to questions that had haunted her for the past eight years. But just knowing what happened wouldn't erase the trauma her friends had endured.

Maria was with Sophia and Graciela. They were at the hospital getting checked out. While their ordeal had just ended, the healing was going to take a long time.

"I was just along for the ride," John demurred. "Rissa deserves the credit."

A flush spread over Rissa's cheeks, and embarrassment flooded her body. "It was teamwork," she countered huskily. She caught his gaze and held it.

"Tell us what went down." That was Connor.

"John jammed Ortega in the back of the head with his crutch." Rissa deflected.

But he was shaking his head. "While Rissa brought down Goon Two."

"Then John disappeared."

"I got the girls to crawl down the mine shaft, so they were out of the way of the gunfire and any potential ricochet."

"And left me alone." She'd been terrified.

"I knew you could handle it." John discreetly threaded his fingers with hers and squeezed. "Rissa shot Goon One and then used his phone to call Jack and the ambulance."

In what was likely a miracle, the guy she shot was alive. Luckily, she'd been able to stop him from dying and he'd face trial for his role in helping Manuel Ortega.

John leaned in and whispered in her ear, "I didn't want to stay on the sideline. But a good teammate recognizes every person's strength and does what's best for the team. I knew you would handle it." And he'd let her. His faith in her filled her with a buoyant light. He believed in her.

Rissa replied, "Thank you."

"Once it was safe, I held a weapon on the unconscious men until help arrived." John finished.

Rissa's stomach roiled. She'd had her hands pressing on Goon One's chest, holding his blood in his body, the scene reminding her so much of the last time when her partner had died.

Except, John had been right. She had handled it. She'd pulled the trigger. Dealt with the noise and the blood, coming full circle.

She hadn't freaked out. She'd trusted her partner and he'd trusted her. It was everything she wanted. And yet, not enough. Not anymore.

Being with John, as a partner and as a lover, had reawakened her zest for life. She'd been living in the shadows afraid to step into the light.

But his actions toward her were contradictory, strained. She wasn't even sure he liked her, let alone—

"To partnership." Her boss, Jillian, winked at Jack and lifted her glass.

There were more congratulatory toasts and back slapping and Rissa tried to fade into the background. Maybe she could just drift away and no one would notice.

JOHN'S SENSE of accomplishment swelled as the accolades and compliments swirled around him and Rissa. Jack's friend at LVPD was in heaven. They had Ortega cold on kidnapping. It was enough to hold him without bail while they executed the search warrants for his businesses.

It was going to take a long time to sort out where all the women in that apartment building had been taken from. But there were several relief organizations who dealt with trafficked women on their way to Vegas to help.

"Well Jack, you certainly know how to throw an eventful pre-wedding vacation," Shelley teased.

Bliss's smile didn't falter but John thought he detected a worried crinkle around her eyes. Jack needed to take care of things before the wedding.

"It's late," Jack said. "We should get out of your hair. Tomorrow you two can move over to the Palazzo for the wedding."

As fast as they arrived, the crowd disappeared.

And Rissa and John were alone.

Rissa moved around the suite, cleaning up glasses and generally avoiding him.

He hadn't had a chance to put his prosthetic on during all the commotion. Using the crutches, he maneuvered so he could corner her against the island. "Hey." John stopped her with a gentle hand on her shoulder. Maybe he'd misread last night but he thought they had taken things to the next level.

Rissa turned and he saw her uncertainty, her longing.

Gazing into her eyes was like freefalling in a HALO jump from thirty thousand feet. His stomach dropped and his heart rate accelerated before settling into a steady, secure rhythm. He tucked a loose strand of hair behind her ear.

Leaning on the crutches for balance, he took the glasses out of her hands and placed them on the counter. Now that they were finally alone, he could wrap his arms around her and hold on.

He pulled her against him and let the thud of her heartbeat calm him. "I am so grateful that you are okay." He brushed a kiss against her temple.

For a moment, she was stiff and unyielding but then

Rissa curled her arms around him and held on tightly. "Right back at you."

Gratitude swelled over him, and he gave in to the need to affirm that she was okay, that he was okay. He slid his hands over her shoulders, trailed up her neck and cupped her face in his palms. He fell into her bottomless gaze and bent his head. The gentle kiss turned frantic as they came together in a rush of passion. Their mouths clashed. John's teeth bumped Rissa's, and their tongues dueled, as desire overwhelmed him. He needed to reaffirm life.

But only with her. "Need you."

"Yes!" Rissa grabbed his hand and tugged him toward his bedroom. She let go so he could thump unevenly toward the king-size bed.

Rissa whipped her shirt over her head, baring her simple cotton bra. Then she took his crutches and placed them carefully next to the bed. His cock rose, arrowing toward her. She caressed him once then pushed him back onto the unmade bed. "Now."

"God, yes." Together, they ripped his shirt off, and he pulled her down between the V of his legs.

Rissa moaned and licked at his chest. "Need you so much." She pushed his shorts down, taking his briefs with them.

"I need a shower." They hadn't had time to clean off after rescuing the women and being interviewed by the police.

"Later." She tore off the rest of her clothes, her magnificent body highlighted by the soft light of the lamp on the end table.

John thumbed her nipples, delighting as they budded under his touch. He cupped her breasts and curled up to lavish them with attention, wanting to slow things down.

But Rissa was nearly frantic with the need to have him inside her. She curled her fingers around his erection and pumped, spreading the drops of pre-cum over his cock.

"Jesus, Riss."

They stopped. Paused.

The weight of the moment hung in the air. He gazed at her, legs spread wide, his cock nestled against her dark curls, her pink-tipped nipples hard buds, her entire body flushed with arousal.

John's cock pulsed, begging for her safe shelter, begging him to take her.

"I was afraid I couldn't do it." Rissa confessed.

"I had faith in you."

"I know." Rissa's knees bracketed his hips, and she lowered onto him as he thrust up inside her at the same time. And he had found home.

THEY LAY in the encroaching darkness wrapped in each other, whispering about their lives, whispering about their hopes and fears for the future. John told Rissa about showing up on his family's doorstep on Thanksgiving, thinking he was going to confront his father and instead finding an instant family.

Rissa told John about losing her nerve after her partner's death, losing her sense of self when she couldn't do her job and was no longer able to do her job after the shooting. Until today when she'd taken back her confidence. When she'd stared down her fear and saved John and the women.

John said, "You were magnificent."

Rissa blushed.

Before he could segue into more personal comments, she lit into him. "What the hell were you thinking?"

"I knew you could handle it."

"What if you'd been wrong?" And oh yeah, there she was. The sweet blushing woman had morphed back into his very own ball buster.

Maybe it was because his mother died and until he'd met his siblings he'd been all alone in the world. But suddenly that craving for contact, for connection with another human being who was there just for him burned in his gut. He knew that was stupid. You couldn't just order up a lover and girlfriend like a guy in line at McDonalds. But even if he had, never in a million years would he have ordered gorgeous with a side a bitchy and vulnerable.

He traced the strong, resolute line of Rissa's jaw. "There she is."

"What? There who is?"

"My BB."

"What does that stand for?"

"You really want to know?"

"Yes."

"Ball Buster." He figured he had a fifty/fifty chance of her jumping out of bed and leaving him.

Rissa wrapped around him like boa constrictor and laughed. The sound shook her body and traveled from her to him. "I like it."

He hugged her tight, one hand tunneled in her messy black hair, and he pressed his other palm flat against the smooth skin of her bare back. Her head burrowed in the crook of his neck, and her lips brushed the sensitive skin behind his ear. "I like *you*."

A shiver worked its way over his spine.

"I like you too." This right here. He wanted this. "I don't know how you feel."

She opened her mouth to speak, and he stopped her. "Let me get this out first."

She nodded.

He said in a rush, "I want what Jack and Bliss have, what Connor and Ava have, what Jess and Colin have, what Riley and Di have."

When he watched his siblings, he could see the love like a physical bond between them and their partners.

Rissa's aquamarine eyes were bright. "I just want *you*. But we'll have to work out logistics."

"I don't want long distance," John blurted out.

"Okay."

"I know you have a job in Washington."

Rissa snorted. "I don't want to be a receptionist anymore."

"How do you feel about moving to California?" His heart thundered when she didn't answer, just stared at him silently. "Okay. Okay. If that doesn't work for you, I'll move to DC."

She pulled back from him. "What about going to work for Jack?"

He shrugged. "I'll go wherever you are."

"But... you just found him and your siblings."

"You are more important."

"But—"

"You overcame your fears to save me." John squeezed her tight. "I would do anything for you."

Rissa grabbed his face with her palms. "I am not easy to live with."

"Not a surprise, babe."

She laughed. "And you don't mind."

"I like you just the way you are."

"Okay." Rissa snuggled against him. "We'll talk to Jack and Jillian and figure it out. It doesn't matter where we land, as long as we're together."

Who would have thought when he'd begun his journey to find his father and exact his revenge, that instead he'd find life? Find a family. Find a purpose. Find Rissa.

He'd gone from nothing to having it all.

He thought about his mother and her final request. She'd wanted him to find his father so he wouldn't be all alone in the world. In a roundabout way, he'd fulfilled her wish even if it wasn't quite what she'd had in mind.

Thanks, Mama.

He wrapped his arms around Rissa and held her close.

He'd always figured he'd go for someone like his mother. Kind, generous, tough but sweet.

And yet, and yet, Rissa fit.

They fit.

EPILOGUE: JACK AND BLISS'S WEDDING

Jack Stone paced the antechamber of the wedding chapel at the Palazzo.

The wedding was about to start. But he was stuck in this small room, waiting and wondering if he was doing the right thing.

Organ music, some song Bliss had picked out, sounded in the background. It was the third song, and he might be imagining it, but the organist started sounding just a little stressed. He knew how she felt. Maybe he'd rushed this. Maybe it wasn't the right time.

He was never unsure of his actions. Ever. Not when he'd left Bliss the first time. Not when he'd quit the Navy to start Global Humanitarian Relief and Stone Consulting. He made a decision and never looked back. But right now, he was considering not only looking but heading back.

"Jack, dude, chill out." Ric Santana—one of his best friends, his commander when he'd been in the SEALs, and Jesus, it was seriously looking on track for Ric to become his stepfather if the past week was any indication—rolled his eyes at him.

Ric clapped his hand on Jack's back and halted his nervous pacing. "It's going to be okay."

"How do you know?" Jack snarled. He knew he was being a dick, but he couldn't shake the thought that he'd made a horrible mistake.

"What's the holdup?" Connor, his youngest brother, barged into the small room. "They're ready to start."

Con took one look at Jack's face and skidded to a halt. "Second thoughts?"

"Fuck no," Jack barked out. He wasn't having second thoughts about marrying Bliss. He was however having second thoughts about his surprise.

They should have just fucking eloped like Bliss wanted.

He should have told her—

"Con." Riley, his other brother, the charming one who'd never met a situation or woman he couldn't finesse, until he'd met Di said, "Shut up."

Jack wanted to smile. Maybe Di's cutthroat ways were rubbing off on smooth-talking Riley's innate need to please.

"Wow, better rein in the charm or Di will never make an honest man out of you," Con razzed Riley. Jack was happy to see that Connor was more at ease than ever with his brothers.

"Uh, yeah." Riley smiled self-deprecatingly. "About that."

Con, Ric, Shane, Jack, and Shelley, his stepmom, stopped. Paused. Waited.

"Di and I…." He put on his most sheepish face. "We got married last week."

"What?" The entire room erupted in a cacophony of surprise and chorus of whys.

"Uh, yeah." Riley flushed. "Di pretty much hates being the center of attention."

But Riley didn't. He thrived on that shit. That's when Jack knew that Riley and Di were really in true love. Only the most precious of emotions would have gotten Ri to forgo the social fun and all the adulation of a wedding. Jack smiled, happy for his brother.

We really should have eloped.

Riley continued, "Turns out, the old man might have passed on his super sperm fertility to me." Riley had always been religious about using contraception because he didn't want to bring any unwanted children into the world like their asshole father.

Riley didn't look upset though. He looked…fucking thrilled. Holy shit. Riley was going to be a daddy. Which meant Jack was going to be an uncle.

"That's…awesome." Happiness overshadowed his own worries for a second.

"You're having a baby?" Shelley's voice rose.

His stepmother was in the groom's room because she was going to walk Jack down the aisle. Even though Shelley was only nine years older than Jack, she'd been mother to all four kids. Now five, because she'd already drawn John Pulaski, his newfound half-brother, into her sphere of influence.

Shel's eyes were wild and not in a good way. "Oh my God, I'm going to be a grandmother?"

"Babe." Ric rubbed his nose along her ear and whispered so that only Shelley and Jack could hear him. "You'll be the sexiest grandmother in Monterey."

Dear God, he was going to start bleeding from his ears.

"Cut that out, Enrique." Jack snapped at his friend and glared at his stepmother. He had known Ric for years. Knew about his sexual exploits. He definitely did not want to have pictures of Ric and Shelley in his brain.

At least Riley's announcement had diverted everyone's attention for a few minutes while Jack had his mini freak-out.

"Yo, mate." Colin Davies, his sister's boyfriend and Jack's buddy from the SAS, burst into the room. "What's the hold-up? According to Jess, your bride is looking very anxious."

Shit, shit, shit.

"You need to talk to her, bro," Con said softly. "Ava told me she's been getting more and more uptight this week. She knows something is going on."

Fuck. He knew he needed to talk to her. But he was suddenly terrified.

John, his newest brother, stepped into the increasingly crowded little room and stood off to the side looking just a little bit shell-shocked. Jack would have been just as uncomfortable if this were his first Stone family rodeo. But in the past year, the chaos of having his entire family around had gotten more familiar. He loved the fact that he'd managed to pull it off. His entire family worked together, and they all lived in Monterey. Sunday dinners at Shelley's house. Vacation together this week--although this had turned into more of a working vacation, between Shelley's stalker issues and John's adventures.

John's gaze sought Jack's and he nodded.

Jack had sent John on this mission because he'd trusted him not to blab the details. At the time Jack had asked his half-brother to help him out, John was the only one without a significant other who might let something slip to Bliss.

But after their mission this week, and the tension between John and Rissa the other night after the rescue, it was clear to Jack that the two of them had gotten close. But

Rissa hadn't said word one to Bliss, so he figured John had kept his secret.

One that now he wasn't sure was such a great idea. His stomach turned.

In fact, what if it was the worst idea he'd ever had?

Bliss Lee stared into the mirror in the bridal suite. Considered all her plans, the flowers, the dress, the reception, the fairy tale she hadn't gotten the first time around. She'd been wrapped up in planning this event for the past few months. Not to mention transferring her workload to her coworkers in DC and beginning the setup to open a West Coast Adams-Larsen office in Monterey.

It had seemed like the perfect solution to her and Jack's logistical issues.

Jillian Larsen, her boss and friend, wanted to expand the business without headaches. So the two businesses were going to merge some facets, and Bliss would be in charge of the office in Monterey. All parts of her life were blending into a perfection that she hadn't even had the imagination to consider.

She'd planned the wedding down to the very last detail. She had the perfect, elegant wedding dress, not too princess-y for a second marriage, a sophisticated column of satin and very subtle lace. Her veil was a sweet confection of lace and tulle.

She'd organized everything perfectly. But the one thing she'd couldn't control was what was going on with the groom.

Her veil gently drifted around her face in a serene cloud. Too bad her stomach hadn't gotten the serenity memo.

Something was wrong.

Wrong with Jack, for sure. Wrong with her and Jack? That, she didn't know.

She'd been feeling uneasy for a while and this past week in Vegas, the threats to Shelley and the mission to rescue Sophia and Graciela aside, she'd known something was off. What if she was making a big mistake?

Moisture threatened her perfect makeup.

Years ago, Jack had left her. Their relationship had been solid, she'd thought. And then he'd decided to join the Navy. Within a month, he was gone and his departure had devastated her. And that had been the end. Until they'd met again last year.

Jillian Larsen, her boss and best friend, stared at her about to overflow eyes. "What's wrong?"

A lump the size of her three-carat emerald engagement ring clogged her throat.

Bliss tried to smile but she was pretty sure it came off as a grimace. "What if he's having second thoughts?"

Jill had heard all about Jack before they'd been reunited on the case to save Maria Torres. "Bliss," Jill said helplessly, but she didn't argue, because Jill had noticed it too.

Jack had been distant and MIA quite a few times over the past week. And when she'd questioned him, he'd blown her off, saying he'd been involved first in Shelley's stalker problems and then John and Rissa's investigation into the abducted girls.

And he'd been strangely quiet after the successful apprehension of the people responsible for their kidnapping and the rescue of the two missing women.

Bliss knew there was more going on.

She distinctly remembered sitting in Jillian's office and

thinking that Jack wasn't just a guy. He was *the* guy. The one who'd ruined her for all other guys.

"I don't know if I can survive it if he dumps me again," Bliss whispered. She didn't want Ava, Connor's girlfriend, or Jess, Jack's sister, to overhear her.

"Come on," Jillian cajoled. "He's completely gone over you."

He had been when they'd first gotten back together but, what if…what if he'd changed his mind? What if he'd suddenly realized that he didn't want to get married? Or even stay together? He'd done it once before. It could happen again.

And it would devastate her.

"What's going on?" Di Lundberg, Riley's girlfriend, wasn't the most outgoing of her newfound family but they'd formed an easy friendship over the past few months. Her fingers brushed over the cream tulle and pearls gently. "So beautiful. Need any help with the veil?"

Bliss blinked away her tears and hoped Di hadn't noticed them. But as she blinked, she noticed the simple gold band on Di's ring finger.

Bliss grabbed her hand and raised a questioning eyebrow. Di flushed a bright red. "We were going to tell everyone tomorrow, after your wedding." Her palm brushed over her abdomen briefly.

Was Di pregnant? Before Bliss could ask, Ava came up on Bliss's other side.

"What's the matter *chica?*" Ava Sanchez smiled wistfully. "You're going to look like a fairy princess," she said softly.

"Girl time," Jess said in a singsong voice. Until she saw Bliss's face, then her smile fell. "What's wrong?"

As if they sensed her teetering on the edge of a breakdown, Jillian and the women from Jack's family, her new family, circled around her like wagons around the campfire.

"It's Jack." Her voice wobbled. Dammit. No way she was ruining her makeup with tears. "You know I'm right."

"It's probably just a bit of nerves." Di didn't pretend away Bliss's fears. "Have you talked to him?"

"Jack loves you!"

"I'm sure it's nothing."

A chorus of other platitudes rang out while everyone tried to put on a happy, unconcerned façade but she knew deep down that they sensed something wrong too.

They were all trying so hard to be upbeat and positive.

"I don't think so." She shook her head miserably. The room went quiet, crickets quiet. No one moved, no one spoke.

"You all felt it." When no one argued, she knew she was right. That's when she decided, fuck it. Bliss had come too far, emotionally and mentally, to go into another marriage with concerns.

No one said a word. Yes, Jill and Rissa were her friends. But she was mostly surrounded by Jack's family who would be loyal to Jack. She understood that he inspired that depth of devotion. Hell, she was devoted to him too. But if it came down to a separation, she knew Jack's family would rally around him. And once again, Bliss would be mostly alone.

It was times like these that she really wished she still had a family. After years of being separated from her dad and sister by the US Marshals' witness protection program, her mom had committed suicide when Bliss was eighteen. She missed her sister. Which in some ways was really silly because she hadn't seen her sister for over half her life. They were teenagers when the family had split up to protect everyone.

Bliss took a shuddering breath and squared her shoulders. She wasn't going to make another mistake. Her first marriage had been strained from the beginning because in the back of her mind she had compared her husband to Jack. She refused to get married to a man who didn't want her.

She swallowed away the lump in her throat and carefully put down the bouquet of white lilies and alstroemeria.

"I need to talk to Jack," Bliss said just as Shelley, Jack's stepmother, walked in the bride's room and said, "Jack needs to talk to you."

Jack strode into the fussy feminine bridal ready room.

He stopped cold when he saw her. She literally took his breath away. Her auburn waves were twisted and piled up on top of her head, revealing the exotic lines of her face. Her high flat cheekbones and tilted green eyes emphasized her Chinese heritage. Her wedding dress hugged her body, accenting her angles and curves. She looked fantastic. Like every fantasy he'd ever had. But when he looked in her eyes, the defeat killed him.

Her face was stoic, and if he didn't know her so well, he'd think she was fine. But after reuniting with her, he'd gotten to where he could read her moods, read her emotions.

"Everyone out," he said without looking away from her.

Bliss didn't move, didn't even twitch. She stood at ease, her hands hanging at her hips waiting. And his heart broke.

Once the door closed quietly, Jack grabbed her around the waist, wrapped her in his arms. "How do you still not know?" His voice was husky.

"What?"

"Fuck, Bliss. You own me." Jack clutched her against him, her passivity more terrifying than her temper. "I'm lost without you."

Tentatively her fingers clutched at the lapels of his tuxedo, and her heart thudded so hard he could feel the beats against his pecs. She'd burrowed her face in his neck. The shuddery sound of her breath slayed him.

"Then what's going on, Jack?"

"I did something." He hesitated. Fuck, he was never hesitant.

She pushed back so that she could look in her eyes and he wanted to drown in her. "Who is she?"

"What the fuck, Bliss?" He growled. "I would never cheat on you."

She relaxed subtly, which was when he realized how much he'd fucked up by keeping this from her. By trying to do something right, he'd done her the worst possible wrong. "I love you. So much." He needed her to understand that. Love was where this had come from.

She smiled tremulously but she didn't reply with an "I love you too."

"I know how much you were missing your family." He was desperate to get her to tell him she loved him back. She wouldn't stop loving him because of this, would she? Hell, his track record with love wasn't what you'd call stellar.

She turned her head away. "Yeah, well, I'm marrying the man of my dreams. Can't have everything."

He got hung up on her statement. Jack gripped her chin in his thick, suddenly clumsy fingers and turned her to face him. "The man of your dreams, huh?"

Warmth and pleasure spread through him like melted

butter. Maybe he didn't need that *I love you* after all. "Hopefully you'll still think so in a few minutes."

She stiffened.

He held up a finger, his heart beating faster than when he'd been under enemy fire. Then, he'd known what to expect. Now, he was winging it and his bright idea a few months ago could turn out to be a total goatfuck.

"Give me one second." He texted on his phone, then strode over to the closed door.

He took a deep breath and prayed he'd done the right thing.

Jack opened the door and stood to the side.

Bliss wondered what was going on. She knew he'd been telling the truth. He loved her. But words were easy. It was actions that mattered. And lately his actions had been furtive and all over the map.

She was a survivor.

She'd survived heartache and loss and isolation. She'd survive this too.

A grizzled older man, broad in the shoulder, a lot of stress lines on his face, stood in the shadowed doorway. Bliss noted the ginger hair liberally threaded with gray. Her mind blanked and her heart stopped beating.

Literally stopped beating.

Everything swooshed down to this one moment. Almost as if she were standing still and the world around her was moving at warp speed, blurry and out of focus, and the only thing she could see clearly was the man in the doorway.

Her throat was so clogged with hope, fear, surprise, she couldn't speak. She blinked, then her eyes flooded with tears, and she forced out a word she hadn't spoken in nearly twenty years.

"Daddy?"

All the blood rushed from her head. Jack had found her father.

There was someone else behind him and she stepped into the room while Jack shut the door behind them and leaned against the white paneled door.

Bliss thought her legs were going to give out.

"Sissy?"

Her sister rushed toward Bliss and threw her arms open wide. "Oh my God. It's you, it's you." Sissy rocked back and forth, her embrace so tight Bliss could barely breathe.

"You're so grown up," Bliss said. Which was silly. She knew that. But in her memories her sister had stopped growing as a young teen.

Her father made his way slowly toward them.

He lifted a trembling hand, an old hand, wrinkled knobby knuckles, then he curled his arms around them both. "My girls." And for the first time in years, her father gave her a hug. "My girls."

Bliss was having a hard time processing. Her brain had shut down. "How, where…."

"You got a special guy there, Joyce."

Joyce? For a second, she didn't know who he was talking to. Then she realized…. "My name is Bliss now."

"Ah, Jack told us." Sissy smiled. "It will take some getting used to."

Her father squeezed them tight. "Bliss. It suits you."

Her sister still hadn't let go. "I missed you so much," she whispered into Bliss's neck.

"I missed you too."

Bliss and her sister broke the hug but kept their arms around each other. Her family.

"I was sorry to hear about your mother, sweetheart." Her father sighed and shoved his hands into his pockets.

Bliss's mouth trembled. "She…had a hard time without you." She brushed off the years of heartache. There was no place for that here. Even though she wanted to break down and sob. All the sorrow and anguish and happiness balled in her throat.

She had given up hope of ever finding her father and sister again. "I can't believe you're here." Bliss lifted a hand to her sister's hair and smoothed her palm over her straight black hair.

She still couldn't process everything. Her father gripped her right hand in his and held on as if she'd disappear for another twenty years if he let go.

"I have so many questions." Bliss laughed through her tears. Guess her makeup was toast after all. But for a much better reason.

"Fire away," her dad said.

"Where do you live?"

"Los Angeles." Daddy asked, "What about you?"

"I was in DC but I'm relocating to Monterey." They were going to be so close.

"So we'll be on the same coast!" her sister said excitedly.

"What do you do?"

Dad smiled. "Bar owner."

Sissy added, "I help out. What about you?"

Bliss paused. Her family's situation had shaped every major decision she'd made in her adult life. But her father and sister seemed so normal. Did she really want to get into her career and life choices now?

"I help people." Was the simple answer.

The organ music started again, seemingly louder than before. The organist had moved from nervous to impatient.

Bliss's gaze shifted to Jack, her heart so full she might burst. He leaned against the door, hyper masculine, his legs crossed, one shoulder elegantly propped against the paneled door, his chin tilted down, the curve of his jaw sharp in the shadows, one hand in his pocket. His overwhelming alpha aura was surrounded by a cloud of uncertainty even as he met her gaze head-on.

"This was what was wrong?" Bliss asked him. This was responsible for the furtive phone calls, late-night meetings, the shifty reasons for cutting out early over many occasions over the past month or so?

He lifted one shoulder and let it drop, his gaze never leaving hers. "I was trying to keep a secret." His lips quirked. "I'm considered pretty good at secrets."

"Next time can you not keep it a secret from me?"

"I wanted to give you a wedding present that money couldn't buy."

Her soon-to-be husband was rolling in money. Which had nothing to do with why she was marrying him. But he could have bought her a small island with a phone call. Instead, he'd given her the one thing she wanted more in the world except for marrying him.

She loved him with all her heart.

"How did you manage to find them?" Bliss had looked for years and even in her line of work, she hadn't been able to find her father and sister. The Marshal system for witness protection had destroyed the records and buried their whereabouts.

"I wondered the same," her dad said slowly. "I looked for years."

Bliss's heart stopped again. "You…looked for me?"

"Of course I did, sweetheart." He wrapped one beefy arm around her neck. "I never stopped looking for you."

Tears brimmed in her eyes. All those years she'd been alone, believing that her father and sister hadn't wanted her.

And the past few weeks believing Jack was getting ready to leave her.

"It wasn't easy," Jack finally answered. "I had a bunch of different contacts combing through years of reports, hoping that I could somehow find a link."

He did this for her. Her throat tightened and speech was impossible.

When she didn't say anything, Jack said, "It finally paid off."

The organ music was getting louder.

Jack cocked his head. "You want me to go tell the staff to chill out for a few minutes?"

Bliss realized all their friends, the employees at the chapel and even her husband-to-be were waiting for her.

She shook her head slowly and pivoted to face her father. "How do you feel about walking me down the aisle?"

Her father's eyes brimmed with happiness and the slight sheen of tears. "You're making me the happiest father in the world."

Jack held out his hand for Bliss's sister. "Come on, I'll take you into the chapel."

Her father crooked his arm, and with a thankful exhale, Bliss threaded her hand through his arm and clung tightly to his elbow.

They walked to the doorway of the chapel in a slow measured pace. When the door opened, every eye turned toward her on her father's arm as Bliss waited for the traditional march.

"You ready?" her daddy asked.

Bliss smiled tremulously and nodded. "I have everything I've ever wanted."

EPILOGUE: THE RECEPTION

Marissa

Jack and Bliss were making the rounds to all the tables at the reception. As far as receptions for millionaires, this one was fairly small, only about thirty people. But Bliss had invited everyone from Adams-Larsen.

John entwined their fingers, his palm solid against hers.

Rissa let a swell of affection roll over as she surveyed the round table holding her friends. There would be time to talk to Jillian when the wedding was over, but she felt totally at peace with her decision to move to California.

John was chatting with Dwayne, their security guy who looked like he could bench press the whole table with everyone sitting on top of it, and Viktor, their quiet medic and weapons master.

Kita, Rissa and Jill gathered around Bliss. She looked radiant.

Jillian slung her arm over Bliss's shoulders. "He found your dad?"

Bliss nodded, her eyes shiny. "Yeah." She shot an adoring glance at Jack.

"You were right." Jillian Larsen, co-founder of ALIAS, white-blond hair with classic Nordic features, squeezed Bliss tight.

"About what?" Kita Kim, their self-defense expert, and Rissa's regular sparring partner, glanced between Jill and Bliss. Kita was always a little reserved around Jill. Maybe because their boss had that very proper manner and Kita was wild and unpredictable and lived to break the rules.

"Jack is *the* guy for Bliss."

Kita snorted. "No such thing as *the one*."

"Wrong." Jillian lifted her chin. "She told me he was the one she never got over. And now I understand see why."

"Can't imagine it." Kita leaned back in her chair and shook her head.

A week ago, Rissa would have agreed with Kita. But now....

"One day." Bliss smiled. "Maybe you guys are next." Bliss had already started in on wanting match everyone.

Jill laughed, but there was a hollow sound to it. "I'm happy for you." She gave a lot to other people and spent all her time working for their clients and looking after her employees.

"Not a chance." Kita smirked, but emotion shadowed her eyes. "No one can keep up with me."

"You never know." Rissa thought about what kind of man could handle Kita. He'd have to be very special. "You deserve the best."

"Yeah, well, I'm perfectly happy by myself." Kita watched the couples congregating on the dance floor. "I'm too busy saving the world to have time for a guy."

Not if she found the right guy. But Rissa kept that to herself.

~

Jack

"Can I steal her for our first dance?" Jack stopped at the table where Bliss was laughing with her friends from Adams-Larsen.

"I'm all yours." Bliss rose and placed her hand in his.

Jack hugged his wife, a thrill swept over him, his *wife*, in his arms as they swayed to the husky crooning from Chad Kroeger singing "How You Remind Me." It might be a little unconventional, but it suited them.

Bliss was a vision in a long column of silky material that clung to her curves, accentuating her stunning body. But as beautiful she was on the outside, Jack was more grateful for her forgiving and generous nature.

She had more than forgiven him for the way he'd handled his gift. He rested his cheek against her hair and breathed in, her jasmine perfume filling his senses. She was his, and he was hers.

She understood him, loved him, in spite of his quirks. As evidenced by her wedding gift to him. A giant bucket was set up in the corner for their wedding gifts. Bliss had requested donations to the various charities who were going to help reintegrate the trafficked women rather than presents.

How had he ever gotten so lucky?

Jack tightened his arms around his wife and surveyed the room.

Jess and Colin were huddled together in the corner talking intimately. Colin had settled in to living in the States. They were still staying with Shelley, but he had a feeling that was going to change soon, especially if Ric ended up moving to Monterey.

"I don't see Shel and Ric." Jesus, he hoped he didn't find them in the coat closet. Again.

Bliss laughed softly. "Pretty sure I saw them heading for the bride room."

Jack shook his head. Jess and Colin were definitely going to be moving out. Fast.

His gaze skimmed over to the bridal party table. Riley was bent over Di as if shielding her from the world around them. His big, scarred palm rested over her belly as he whispered something in her ear. A soft, uncharacteristically sweet smile softened her face and her blue eyes sparkled.

It was the most content he'd ever seen his brother.

Finally, his gaze moved to John and Rissa. They were watching the first dance, not touching but the bond between them was palpable.

Jack was so thankful that John had had enough fire to hunt down the manwhore. If he hadn't, they would have never met. "Some days I think I should thank my father."

Bliss smoothed her hand over his shoulder, her attempt at comfort. "You definitely have a unique family."

"I'm giving John a share of the company." He didn't think she'd care, but now that they were married, and damn, did he love that, he supposed he should clue Bliss in on financial decisions.

"I figured you would." There was nothing but approval in her gaze.

Life now surpassed his vision when he'd made the decision to form Global Humanitarian Relief and Stone Consulting and bring his siblings all together. It had been a dream, the business founded in great principles, but the family piece had been more fantasy than practicality. They'd had their ups and downs, but now the result of those seeds was growing and getting bigger and better than he'd ever even imagined.

He swung Bliss around, considered the clutch of employees from Adams-Larsen at the other table. Marsh Adams was conspicuously absent again. Bliss's father and sister were sitting with Jillian Larsen, Kita Kim, Dwayne Lameko, and Viktor Kuznets. "Are you going to miss them?"

He didn't know her crew well, but they clearly had a strong foundation.

"I will." She sighed against his shoulder. "But not as much as I missed you."

His heart expanded.

Con and Ava sat at the other end of the bridal table. Con was playing with Ava's fingers as they chatted with Maria, who had come out of her shell in the past few weeks. Having a hand in catching the people responsible for kidnapping her and her friends all those years ago agreed with her.

"What do you think about Maria going to work for Adams-Larsen?"

Bliss tilted her head back. "Such a sweet talker."

Jack blushed. Actually blushed. But he couldn't help it. "I'd just like to see her settled…and happy."

A smile curved Bliss's face. "You want to take care of her."

Jack blustered. "I'm just trying to make sure she's got a future."

"It's a trait I really admire." She bussed his lips. "It's…sweet."

"Sweet?" There was a hint of outrage in his tone. "I am *not* sweet."

"Don't worry, big guy." Bliss pressed another kiss to his mouth. "It will be our secret."

Whatever. He was not sweet.

"So?" he asked belligerently.

"I think it's a great idea."

Jack nodded. One down. But really, they could talk business another day.

"It's our day."

Bliss rested her head on his shoulder, her hand clasped in his as they swayed to the music.

His thumb rubbed the simple gold band around his ring finger.

He liked it. No. He *loved* it. The unadorned ring proclaimed to the whole world that they belonged together. "I'm yours."

"Yes, you are."

"And you're mine." That was just the way he wanted it. "Forever."

What does Adams-Larsen do if it isn't image consulting? Check out Kita Kim's story in Stalked (ALIAS #1), the first book in the ALIAS series. An opposites attract romantic suspense romance: rule breaker, Kita, has to team up with a very uptight, rule follower US Marshal to protect a federal judge with deadly secrets.

Thank you, thank you, thank you for reading the final Family Stone book, Cold As Stone!

p.s. Would you like to know when my next book is available? You can sign up for my new release email list/newsletter at Lisa's Confidants. I send newsletters about twice a month and feature sales, giveaways, and bonus short stories.

ACKNOWLEDGMENTS

The list of usual suspects who are always there for me:

Adrienne Bell and LGC Smith for our regular writing dates and moral support.

The Pens: Gigi Pandian, Rachael Herron, Juliet Blackwell, Sophie Littlefield, and Mysti Berry for the friendship and fun over the last five years. I am so happy to know you!

For my pal, Cecilia Gray, who is always willing to open her home for a mini-break retreat or head to a hotel for writing weekends with copious amounts of room service and plotting.

To LJ at Mayhem Cover Creations. Thank you for the beautiful covers!

And lastly, I'm so pleased to have the chance to work with a new editor, Deb Nemeth. Her input and corrections helped me immensely. I'm looking forward to continuing our working relationship!

AUTHOR'S NOTE

I took a little creative license for this story. There is no such service called Backdoor. There is a service BackPage which did in fact take over the Craigslist Adult Services listings, however I really, really didn't want to give the site any web traffic so I chose to create an imaginary site.

Human trafficking is everywhere. And could in fact be going on in your hometown. Please be aware and speak up if something seems suspicious.

For more information on how to spot and combat trafficking visit the State Dept.
http://www.state.gov/j/tip/id/help/
There are organizations to help victims of human trafficking. One in particular is Thistle Farms.
http://thistlefarms.org/
Finally, Michael Stokes is a real person. He is an amazing photographer and shoots many former military amputees. Do a search for him on Twitter and Facebook to check out his photos. http://michaelstokes.net/

ALSO BY LISA HUGHEY

Family Stone Romantic Suspense

Stone Cold Heart, (Jess, Family Stone #1)

Carved in Stone (Connor, Family Stone #2)

Heart of Stone (Riley, Family Stone #3)

Still the One (Jack, Family Stone #4)

Jar of Hearts (Keisha & Shane, Family Stone #5)

Queen of Hearts (Shelley, Family Stone #6)

Cold as Stone (John, Family Stone #7)

Family Stone Box Set (Stone Cold Heart, Carved in Stone, Heart of Stone, Still the One, & Jar of Hearts)

ALIAS

Stalked (ALIAS #1)

Hunted (ALIAS #2)

Vanished (ALIAS #3)

Saved (ALIAS #3.5)

Deceived (ALIAS #4)

Compromised (ALIAS #5) Coming Soon

Black Cipher Files Romantic Suspense

The Encounter, A Prequel to Blowback

Blowback

Betrayals

Burned

Dangerous Game

Black Cipher Files Box Set (includes Blowback, Betrayals, and Burned)

Snow Creek Christmas

Love on Main Street: A Snow Creek Christmas – 7 Author anthology

One Silent Night (from Love on Main Street)

Miracle on Main Street (standalone novella)

The Nostradamus Prophecies

View To A Kill #1

Never Say Never #2

Billionaire Breakfast Club

His Semi-Charmed Life (Billionaire Breakfast Club #1)

Everything He Wants (Billionaire Breakfast Club #2)

She Feels Like Home (Billionaire Breakfast Club #3)

Sideways (Tracy's story is part of Sarina Bowen's Speakeasy series)

His Road To Paradise coming in 2021

His Dirty Little Secret

ABOUT THE AUTHOR

About Lisa

USA Today Bestselling Author Lisa Hughey started writing romance in the fourth grade. That particular story involved a prince and an engagement. Now, she writes about strong heroines who are perfectly capable of rescuing themselves and the heroes who love both their strength and their vulnerability. She pens romances of all types—suspense, paranormal, and contemporary—but at their heart, all her books celebrate the power of love.

She lives in Cape Ann Massachusetts with her fabulously supportive husband and two very skittish rescue tuxedo kittens.

Beach days, hiking, and traveling are her favorite ways to pass the time when she isn't plotting new ways to get her characters to fall in love.

Lisa loves to hear from readers and has tons of places you can connect with her. It's a wonder she gets any writing done at all....

Be Lisa's Friend on Facebook
Sign Up for Lisa's Confidants
Visit Lisa on the Web
Follow Lisa on Pinterest
Follow Lisa on Instagram
Email Lisa

Kita Kim took a direct hit across the chin.

Only the heavy padding saved her from a knockout blow. Her ears rang and white stars sparkled in her vision. That was what she got for letting her mind wander, even for a moment.

Kita shook off the daze. She was trying to train Hannah Smith to defend herself. The goal was to get Hannah to engage if one of her nieces was being attacked by their father. But if she hadn't fallen into that kick, it would have lacked the force needed to really hurt her.

Hannah got in a kick to Kita's thigh. She'd probably have a bruise, but the woman hadn't used near enough force to take down a two-hundred-fifty-pound man.

"Do it again. You have to kick hard enough to hurt a guy who weighs a lot more than you do." She purposely infused her voice with perkiness, leaving out the frustration.

Hannah nodded, setting her mouth and crouching into a defensive stance. Her eyes, lost in a sea of delicate, purpling skin, glowed with anger. Her muscles trembled with rage, but her matchstick arms would be no problem for the bulk and sheer power of her abusive brother-in-law bent on attack.

Unless Kita could get Hannah ready to defend against her attacker slash abuser slash brother-in-law, he would crush this woman, just as he had crushed Hannah's sister. At least, that was what they believed. Tammy Donner had disappeared. After a cursory investigation by the local police, Frank Donner had been cleared. He insisted that his wife had run away and left him and their three daughters.

But Hannah and Kita knew the truth. Frank Donner had killed his wife. And if Kita couldn't get Hannah to defend herself and her nieces, she was worried he would kill Hannah too.

Somehow Kita had to get Hannah to embrace her rage. Whip her into a vengeance frenzy. Or at the very least, induce her to not curl up into a defensive ball.

Because Kita's boss, Jillian Larsen, had refused to help Hannah. Even though Hannah Smith and her nieces were just the type of clients usually helped by the agency Jillian had cofounded.

Adams-Larsen Inc. and Associates—publicly an exclusive PR firm—was privately a relocation specialist agency.

"We don't break the law," Jillian had said to Kita emphatically.

Because Adams-Larsen, or ALIAS, as she and her coworkers affectionately called it, skated on the edges of legality. While nothing they did was outright illegal, there were definitely blurred lines. At the end of the day, they saved people. And Kita loved being part of justice for those wronged.

Which is why this situation sucked big hairy donkey balls. Hannah Smith was in serious trouble.

Frustration bubbled in Kita's stomach. She hated when abusers picked on someone weaker. *Asshole.*

She could take down the brother-in-law with ease. But Frank Donner wasn't going after her. And Kita could only offer Hannah lessons while she wasn't on a case. If Kita received a new assignment, she'd have to cut back on training Hannah.

Kita held up her arm and rubbed her nose through the concealing face mask.

Jeez, she was ripe. The earthy odor of sweat steamed in the padded assailant suit. Her powder scent deodorant, which had worn off an hour ago, left her less than fresh. Major body odor wafted into her nose along with the unhealthy scent of Hannah Smith's fear.

Normally Kita reveled in this type of workout but Hannah's obvious discomfort hit at Kita's consciousness and her muscles were rigid with impotent frustration. Tension ratcheted up with every sobbing breath Hannah took. The threat to Hannah was real and immediate, not some faceless, nameless bogeyman, but a man who had and could kill. Even if no one but Hannah and Kita believed it. But Jillian Larsen didn't care that Kita believed Frank Donner was a killer.

"Kita." Jill had gentled her voice. "I understand your aversion to authority. It's a good part of the reason we hired you. I even understand your frustration."

Kita had rubbed at the abnormal bump on her wrist, the break that hadn't quite set properly when she was seventeen.

Jillian didn't always play by the rules either, but she couldn't understand something she'd never experienced. Kita knew in her improperly-healed, ached-when-it-rained wrist that Hannah Smith was in mortal danger.

Adams-Larsen had the means and the contacts to save Hannah and her three nieces. But they weren't going to.

"Again." Kita prepped to attack the slight woman.

The bulky padding made Kita look like the Michelin Man on steroids. Due to years of training, she could move with a fair amount of agility, probably more than Hannah's brother-in-law possessed. But Hannah needed to learn to counter the violent threat. She needed to work past her fear and get angry.

Kita rushed Hannah, roaring, trying to scare her, trying to shake her.

Within seconds Hannah leapt out of Kita's path, then twirled with a roundhouse kick to Kita's back. Kita rolled, then swept Hannah's feet out from underneath her, and she hit the padded floor with a thud. Kita jumped to her feet and leaned over her.

The woman lay on the mat, her eyes closed, her cheeks gaunt and the yellowed bruising, from the black eye before this one, apparent in the bright florescent lighting.

"You okay?"

Hannah's chest heaved. Through the entire training session she hadn't said a word. Not once had she cried out, even when Kita had struck a blow.

A single tear trailed down the side of Hannah's face and pooled in her ear. Kita's heart shattered at the defeat pulsing off this woman in waves.

"How am I ever going to do this?" Hannah's voice shook and she still hadn't opened her eyes.

Kita refused to give up.

"Right now is when you strike," Kita said fiercely. "Right now, with your heavy booted foot, you kick as hard as you can at his crotch."

Sweat poured down Kita's back, and her hair matted to her skull underneath the face mask and extra padding.

"Kick me as hard as you can," Kita demanded. "Don't hesitate. You won't hurt me." The crotch had been reinforced to protect the suit wearers, usually men, from the debilitating blows.

"You're so strong," Hannah whispered. "You don't understand how hard this is."

A heavy, gaping crater swallowed Kita's heart. Air stuck in her throat, and her lungs resisted her breath so sharply the gasp hurt. She grasped Hannah's shoulders. She hadn't always been strong. And she knew exactly how fucking hard this was for Hannah.

"You do not have to be a victim."

Hannah whimpered. Kita knew she wasn't hurting the woman, she was barely holding on to her.

"I can't do this."

"You *can.*"

Kita wanted to rage at the system that let a violent offender go free to terrorize his family, the very people he should protect and keep safe.

But she knew, better than anyone, that life wasn't always fair. And the only one you could count on to protect you—was you.

For a moment she wished Marsh Adams— her friend, her mentor, the man who'd showed her these moves when she'd been facing her own demons—was here. As Jillian's partner, Marsh was the reason Kita worked for the agency. But Marsh was MIA these days, out on assignment, and no amount of wishing was going to bring him back.

"You can do this." Kita leaned forward in a lunge, holding out her hand, waiting for Hannah to grasp it so she could pull the tiny woman to her feet.

"He's going to kill me." The defeated slump of Hannah's shoulders sparked a resounding denial. No way was she going to let Hannah's asshole brother-in-law win. She'd do whatever it took to make sure Hannah and the children were safe.

"Not if I have anything to say about it."

The rumble of the employee garage door vibrated through the gym floor and the protective mats, shimmying up Kita's body to stop in the region of her heart. Adrenaline flooded her. It was the middle of the morning and as far as she knew everyone at the office was accounted for.

Except Marsh.

But ever since an incident in this building last month, the staff had been a little on edge.

Could just be someone in the field coming in for tech or ops help. Although she didn't have any appointments on her calendar. Could it be Dwayne or Victor, coming back from a relo early?

The first set of locks disengaged. Then the second door lock buzzed, the click resoundingly loud in the sudden silence of the sparring room. Hannah cowered on the floor as Kita shifted to watch the mirrors lining the wall and to observe who entered the facility.

A transparent bullet-resistant wall, made of layers of glass and polycarbonate, isolated Kita and Hannah from any threat in the hallway. The only way into the sparring room was through the password-protected entrance to the locker room on the other side of the building. The basement had been revamped to accommodate the sparring room, showers, lockers and the totally indulgent steam room.

Hannah grabbed her hand and Kita hefted her up to standing with one forceful jerk. "Again."

Kita split her attention between Hannah and the mirrors.

Hannah smoothed down the material of her yoga pants and dropped back into a defensive stance. Kita nodded in approval. *Yeah, that's it. Kick my ass.*

The steel-reinforced door opened slowly. The shadows beyond the entrance to the garage were dark and somehow ominous. Her tension ramped up as she readied to attack Hannah, while her brain shifted into higher gear, preparing to defend Hannah against danger. Which was stupid because whoever was coming through the door would have already had to go through several security checkpoints before being allowed access to the building. Adams-Larsen took their security seriously. No one who didn't belong breached the facility.

No one.

And since the shooting last month, security had been tighter than ever.

Kita's heart thumped loudly in her chest. *The ba-bump, ba-bump* a rapid percussion, as her hearing preternaturally heightened while she waited for whatever, whoever, was coming.

A silver-haired man with broad shoulders and an imperious bearing—something about his demeanor so arrogant the very air around him seemed to be holding its breath—stepped through the door. The single halogen light illuminated his face with startling clarity. She'd never officially met him, but, she knew who he was. She'd seen pictures in Marsh's office.

The judge. Marsh's father.

In the shadows behind him another man paused in the doorway. Ignoring the workout room and sparring women, the judge strode down the hallway like he owned the place.

Hannah kicked out and Kita twisted carefully to block the kick to her thigh. "You need to hit right on the knee."

Hannah nodded and crouched again.

Something in the movement of the second man drew her gaze back as he entered. He pulled the reinforced door closed behind him. The overhead halogen beam highlighted the almost blue-black of his hair and emphasized his broad shoulders. He kept his face turned away from the observation windows, staying in the shadows.

Not Marsh. It had been stupid to hope that Marsh was coming. It had been what felt like forever since he'd been in the office.

Apprehension shivered over Kita's spine. Hannah shifted so she was slightly behind Kita.

Ironic. Both the man above her and the woman behind her were hiding.

For a moment, the man paused. He had stepped into the light, head tilted down, watching the defensive tableau, his pale blue eyes piercing, glowing with intensity. Kita felt the man's regard like an almost physical caress. Her visceral reaction to the quick assessment was confusing, unwanted.

As if a rush of pheromones had drop-loaded into her system and made a beeline toward her female parts.

Her five-ten body was cocooned in the padded assailant suit, her breasts smashed and wrapped to protect from blows, and her ombre blond ponytail encased in the watch cap underneath a large padded helmet. Sex should be the last thing on her mind.

I

EXCERPT FROM STONE COLD HEART

Family Stone #1 Jess

In the early evening dusk, Jess Stone lay on her stomach in the twenty foot high rubble of a demolished church, underneath a black and gray city-scape tarp intended to camouflage her position. A sharp-edged chunk of debris dug into her lower rib cage, the scope of the Remington M24 cool and familiar against her face.

Her standard uniform of jeans, running shoes, and plain black t-shirt rendered her just another anonymous and transient relief worker...which she was actually. A black baseball cap hid her distinctive multi-hued blonde hair. The paper mask kept out the contaminated dust from the destroyed buildings but did little to stem the overwhelming stench of decaying bodies.

Tanks rumbled through the destroyed coastal town, their public address system blasting warnings for citizens to stay in their homes, curfew was in effect. The threat was a joke. Ninety percent of the people in the town didn't have homes left. Those who did were terrified to go back inside. In the fetid, humidity choked air, the tent cities erected in the parks and on the beach were seething masses of the injured and shock struck.

The substandard construction in the small country had never been enough to withstand the angry might of Mother Nature. Buildings had toppled like a stack of Tinkertoys, and left crumbling cement walls with twisted rebar poking out of the jagged ruins like a skeletal hand.

Trapped in the concrete pieces that littered the ground, the heat from the tropical day seared through her thin sturdy clothing. The stank of the raw sewage that ran in rivulets through the streets overpowered the salt-laden breeze off the ocean. People, covered with the grit of pulverized buildings and humans, shuffled along with blank vacant stares. Two weeks after the quake, still in shock, their lives decimated first by nature and then kicked and beaten by the ineffectiveness of a flawed relief system. Hundreds of humanitarian agencies had descended on the population duplicating efforts and yet completely missing the need in other areas. The government was ostensibly trying to coordinate the effort, however the mass chaos was undeniable.

Through the Leupold Ultra M3 fixed power sight, she tracked the movements of Henri LeRoy, leader of this tiny island nation, violator of human rights and dignity, and all around poor excuse for a human being.

Sickness roiled in her stomach. The power bar she'd eaten for breakfast threatened to add to the rubble pile as she tried to figure out how in the hell she'd ended up here. Back behind a sniper rifle with the power over life and death trembling in the muscles of her right trigger finger.

Dammit. When she'd decided to take control of her life and quit the FBI, she hadn't wanted to do this anymore.

She'd wanted to be a simple relief worker. She'd wanted to connect with her family, brothers and mother.

But that bitch, fate, had slapped her upside the head and now here she was, where she'd sworn she never wanted to be again. Looking through the scope of a high-powered rifle, with a crystal clear head shot and a murky sense of right and wrong.

With little fanfare, she could blast LeRoy's brain matter all over the silk-covered walls and the antique Louis the XIV scrolled chairs in the receiving room of his ridiculously elegant weekend mansion which, since built properly, had sustained minimal damage. Her muscles twitched with the knowledge and acceptance that with one slow slide of her finger, the despotic, amoral leader would be history.

Jess didn't want to kill him, didn't want to be directly responsible for another death. She didn't want this choice. She'd given up this kind of life. She'd left the FBI after a series of high stress cases to get away from the doubt and guilt that had crippled her. To make her own decisions about right and wrong rather than carry out the commands of her bosses.

But if Henri LeRoy lived, chances were astronomical that many other citizens would die.

And yeah, she'd probably been manipulated into this. Actually no probably about it. Assassination had not been listed as one of her duties when she'd joined Global Humanitarian Relief. Damn her brother anyway.

But now all she could do was lay here in the desecrated remains of the former church and hope that her special skill set wouldn't be needed.

Fortunately, she was secondary backup.

And unless several things went horribly wrong, she would break down her weapon, get back to the relief aid encampment, back to actually helping people, and be out of here without ever firing her rifle.

Then she could hand out seed packets to her heart's content and figure out what she was going to do next. If she'd stay with GHR and her brothers, or go. First, she had to get through the next two hours.

But if something did go wrong...she prayed that if she was called upon, she could make the right decision. Make the shot. Cold zero.

Family Stone Romantic Suspense
   Stone Cold Heart:
   Jess Stone, former FBI sniper, always felt like the kid who looked in the candy store window but could never afford to go in. But on a humanitarian mission to aid an earthquake ravaged country, finally she finds a place where she fits, in Colin Davies' arms, and working for Global Humanitarian Relief, her big brother's company. But can the former SAS thaw Jess's stone cold heart?

Carved in Stone:
   Connor Stone has always been odd man out in his family. Not the oldest, not the most charming, he'd had a lock on the youngest until another half-sibling came to live with them, so he raised hell in his youth. Con knows now the only way to redeem himself is with deeds, not words and sets out to prove once and for all he is worthy of the Stone family. When his older brother asks him to take care of business, Con finally will have redemption he craves. Except when Ava Sanchez, his brother's assistant, is threatened, he

must choose between saving the girl or protecting his family. Will his choice bring him love or break his heart?

Heart of Stone:

Riley Stone is the handsome brother, the charming one. Everyone who meets him compares him to his father, which in his mind is not a compliment. But he's never met a woman he couldn't charm, until he meets Di, an acerbic, smart-mouthed, passionate activist who has no time for him or his charm. On the run, in the midst of danger, the blistering passion they share explodes. Can these two opposites find common ground, or will Di smash Riley's stone heart?

Still the One:

Jack Stone, former Navy SEAL, and oldest Stone sibling is determined to keep his family strong. Family is everything. So he starts Global Humanitarian Relief and Stone Consulting to do some good and keep his family together. But when he has to team up with his old flame, Bliss, on a missing persons case, an evil threatens him, his family and the one woman he could never forget and doesn't want to let go. Can these two former lovers put aside past hurts and heal their hearts?

Jar of Hearts:

Prickly Keisha Johnson has the hots for Shane Washington. But she's not about to reveal her inner soft heart to the player pilot and open herself up to hurt, until a favor to their boss sends them undercover and under the covers. Can she trust his sensual attention or will he shatter her fragile heart?

Queen of Hearts:

Ric Santana is in Las Vegas for his friend's wedding and some much needed R & R. But the vacation turns awkward when he discovers his smoking hot, one night stand is actually his pal's stepmother. When Shelley's life is threatened, Ric doesn't hesitate to step into the role of bodyguard and protector. But as Ric grows closer to Shelley, he can't help but wonder, can he save her life or will they be too late for love?